THE HAUNTING OF GREY HILLS
What Dread Hand

JENNIFER SKOGEN

EPIC
Press

What Dread Hand
The Haunting of Grey Hills: Book #3

Written by Jennifer Skogen

Copyright © 2016 by Abdo Consulting Group, Inc.

Published by EPIC Press™
PO Box 398166
Minneapolis, MN 55439

Cover design by Dorothy Toth
Images for cover art obtained from iStockPhoto.com
Edited by Melanie Austin

LIBRARY OF CONGRESS CATALOGING-IN-PUBLICATION DATA

Skogen, Jennifer.
What dread hand / Jennifer Skogen.
p. cm. — (The haunting of Grey Hills ; #3)
Summary: What really happened during the fire of 1966? Go back in time and see
the famous tragedy through the eyes of student Henry Grey, and history teacher
Lorna Evans. Henry's uncle, Principle Grey, is teaching Henry to fight ghosts, but is
there something his uncle isn't telling him? Lorna returns to Grey Hills after inheri-
ting her father's house. She also inherits an urn of her grandfather's ashes, which may
contain more than first meets the eye.
ISBN 978-1-68076-031-6 (hardcover)
1. Ghosts—Fiction. 2. High schools—Fiction. 3. Supernatural—Fiction.
4. Haunted places—Fiction. 5. Young adult fiction. I. Title.
[Fic]—dc23
2015932721

For everyone who let me see their 1960s yearbooks. You all looked great!

Prologue

Halloween, 2016

When Henry Grey pressed the knife to Macy's throat, he could feel her pulse through the steel blade. It was like a message sent down a telegraph wire, pounding out one clear word over and over again. *Why?*

Henry couldn't remember if the world had felt like this when he was alive. Had the light of the moon always throbbed in his head like the sound of distant waves? If he let himself, he would fly apart into a million pieces of nothingness.

He could feel Macy's mind pulling at him,

scratching at whatever threads held what remained of his consciousness in one place. Henry wanted to let her do it. He wanted to disappear.

She was strong. In the instant before Henry sank the blade deep into Macy's throat, he felt himself begin to unravel. As strong as she was, Henry was stronger. He held her even tighter to his chest, as though her body would keep his own semblance of a body from unspooling into the night air.

"Shhh," Henry whispered into her ear. "It's almost over."

The Door was hungry. That was something he hadn't understood when he was still alive. The Door wasn't just a door. It was a mouth.

Macy's death would be enough. Henry hadn't been sure it would work until he felt the Door ripple behind him. He left her there, bleeding into the dirt, clutched in the arms of the boy who had followed her there. Henry didn't know what the boy's name was, but he was weeping.

Henry had lied to Macy about many things,

but the Door wasn't one of them. As soon as he stepped through the Door, Henry would leave behind the crumbled, burned-out school and the silent screams that seemed to hang in the air like stirred-up dust.

He would forget.

Chapter One

1966

Lorna didn't realize at first that she was holding her grandfather's ashes.

She had woken up well before dawn and couldn't get back to sleep. She'd been having that dream that she was buried alive again.

When Lorna finally wrenched herself awake, she took several deep breaths. The dream slowly faded. She ripped off the sheets, which had gotten wrapped around her legs while she was sleeping. Even after Lorna was fully awake, it had felt like the walls of the house were shrinking around her.

She stared at the ceiling of her childhood room, trying in vain to fall back asleep. Lorna would have counted the cracks in the paint like she used to do when she was a child, but it was too dark to see them.

When she first moved home to Grey Hills after her father's death, Lorna discovered that her old room had been filled with boxes. The boxes themselves weren't hard to move. They were mostly full of newspapers or carelessly wrapped knickknacks that had been her mother's prized possessions. It was what the boxes represented that bothered her. Her room, which used to be kept clean and ready for her to visit while her mother was alive, was now a junk room.

It wasn't only Lorna who had been set aside. She could easily picture her father taking her mother's porcelain cats and glass-eyed dolls off their shelves and hiding them away. Lorna didn't know if he had done that because it was too painful to have constant reminders of his dead wife or if he had just always hated her things.

Lorna lay in bed for almost forty-five minutes, willing herself to go back to sleep. The bed seemed so much smaller than when she was a girl, though she couldn't imagine that she had grown an inch since she was fifteen years old. She had purchased new sheets and pillows right after she moved back home. The mattress was the same, however, and seemed to sink in slightly at the center, as though the ghost of Lorna's childhood had refused to get out of bed.

Finally, once the dim light of early morning began to—not exactly brighten—but dispel some of the dark from her room, Lorna decided to get up. It was too early to eat breakfast, and the house itself had killed much of her appetite. She had scrubbed the refrigerator from top to bottom, but there were some stains that she could not get out. There were also mice, she was certain, who rummaged through the cupboards at night.

If Lorna had unlimited time and money, she would burn this house to the ground and build another, more modern house in its place. Something clean, and spacious, with one wall made entirely of windows to catch the southern sun.

Since it was still far too early to leave for the first day at her new job, Lorna decided to finally sort through a few of the last boxes that she had been ignoring. That was probably why she hadn't been able to sleep: the job. Just when she had inherited a house in her old home town, a history position had opened up at her old high school. The job, which should have been an exciting new chapter in her life, had been looming over her like an oncoming storm cloud.

Lorna figured this must be what stage fright was like, though she had never been an actress. She had also never actually taught at a public high school, but she remembered the walls of the classrooms at Grey Hills like they were an old amputated limb that ached every now and again. This job was her one chance to take root in this new, old life of hers. She couldn't mess it up.

When Lorna was unpacking a third box, she found the blue vase. It was wrapped in a faded dishtowel and had been packed beside a few china cats and a stack of Kennedy plates that Lorna had immediately decided to give away to a charity shop. As she unwrapped the vase, Lorna tried to remember if she had ever seen it holding the long-stemmed irises her mother had loved. Once she had it uncovered and held it up for inspection, Lorna realized that it wasn't a vase at all.

It was an urn.

For a terrible moment Lorna thought she might be holding her mother—that her father had lied about burying his wife in the cemetery up on Myrtle Street and had kept them hidden in a box all these years. But when Lorna looked closer, she realized that she had seen this urn before. It contained her grandfather's ashes. Lorna remembered her father bringing out the urn when she was very young, and telling her how her grandpa had died when he (Lorna's father) was only seventeen.

"An accident," her father had said. He had been drinking, of course, and had to wipe a few sloppy tears off his face. It was years before Lorna realized that her father had meant *the* Accident. The 1916 explosion that had killed eleven construction workers, including her own grandfather.

Lorna carried the urn into the kitchen, which had the best light from wide, newly cleaned windows. She turned the urn over, looking for the inscription that she faintly remembered would be on the bottom. *W. C. Evans*. William Carter. Her grandfather.

She ran her finger along the seal at the top, wondering what would happen if she pried open the lid. Lorna had never seen a dead person before, not even her mother. Her dad hadn't waited for Lorna to come home before he had her mother cremated and buried.

Lorna didn't blame her father—not for that part of it at least. Lorna hadn't actually wanted to see her mother's body. Not like that. Not bruised and broken by the car accident that should have killed him instead—her father. He was the one who had been drinking when he took a left-hand turn without looking, and an oncoming car had slammed into the passenger door. Her mother's door.

No one told her that her father was drunk, but she just knew it. When was he ever sober?

She considered the lid of the urn. If she reached inside, would her grandfather's ashes feel like the ones from the wood stove? It had been Lorna's job, when she was a child, to clean the hearth by scooping out the ashes. Her father told her that if she didn't, the ashes would grow too deep and smother the fire like a snowdrift.

Would her grandfather's ashes feel different? Would her fingers just *know*, somehow, that they used to be a person?

Lorna didn't really intend to open the urn. She often imagined things she never intended to do, like cutting her hair into a bob and hitchhiking across the country. A friend of Lorna's had dropped out of college and did just that—she lived in a commune in Oregon somewhere and probably had contracted syphilis by now. Or had ten children. Lorna wasn't sure which would be worse.

Lorna rinsed the outside of the urn in the sink and wiped it clean with a fresh towel. *What to do with Grandfather?* she wondered, setting the urn on the kitchen counter.

Lorna still had plenty of time before school started, but she didn't want to rush. As she always did when starting a new school year, Lorna had planned out her morning to the minute. She had washed her hair the night before and placed her books and papers in her worn leather satchel and set that by the front door. Lorna had even laid out her clothes—draping her corduroy skirt and dark sweater over a wooden chair in the hall just outside her bedroom. A few days earlier, Lorna had timed the drive to Grey Hills High School, so she knew exactly what time she had to pull out of the driveway.

She was about to walk out the front door when she remembered that she had left her father's car keys on the kitchen counter. Usually Lorna could imagine exactly what the day ahead would hold. Her old job at a boarding school in New York had lent a sort of methodical similarity to the days. She knew that eventually her new life in Grey Hills would fall into a comfortable routine. Right now, however, Lorna felt like her skin was vibrating at the wrong frequency. She frowned as she walked back to the kitchen, each step wrong—unaccounted for.

As Lorna grabbed the keys and turned to go, she felt her elbow connect with something solid. Even as she spun back around—hands held out before her, fingers splayed—Lorna knew it was too late. The urn hit the kitchen tile and shattered into a thousand blue splinters.

Lorna closed her eyes. She didn't want to see the ashes after all.

Finally, she forced herself to open her eyes. It

was a mess. Lorna stood over the broken urn, and stared at the thin layer of ash that now covered the kitchen floor.

Shit.

She held her breath—Lorna did *not* want to inhale her grandfather. After standing there for about thirty seconds, blinking in frustration at the scene before her, Lorna got to work. She found a dustpan and broom in the laundry room, and an empty cookie jar in a kitchen cupboard. Quickly, Lorna swept the ash and the broken shards of urn into the dust bin.

Lorna soon realized that what she had assumed were more pieces of broken urn were actually small, pale chunks of bone. Her stomach turned when she heard the *clink, clink* of the broken urn, and bones, while she gently poured her grandfather's remains into the ceramic cookie jar.

When she had saved most of . . . him . . . Lorna wiped up the residual film of ash with a damp cloth, then threw the cloth into the garbage. She couldn't possibly use it to dry the dishes after it had been covered with pieces of a dead man.

Lorna washed her hands—turning the faucet as hot as it could go—and then walked gingerly across the kitchen floor on her way out. When she reached the edge of the kitchen, where the tile met the ugly, brown carpet, Lorna's heart sank. There, caught in a depression between tiles, was a single shard of bone.

She almost stepped over the bone and kept walking, but then she paused, scooping up the fragment of bone. It felt light in her hand, as though it were hollow. Almost like a bird's bones would feel, she imagined. She supposed that's what fire did—it stripped a person of substance. Made them weightless.

Lorna's chest felt too full. She took a deep breath and blinked back the first prickle of tears. Then she slipped the sliver of bone—which was smaller than her pinky nail—deep into the pocket of her gray corduroy skirt and walked out the door.

Chapter Two

Henry Grey drove to school in his shiny black car. The Rolling Stones' "Paint It Black" was on the radio. He didn't sing along, but he drummed his fingers on the steering wheel, feeling the beat of the song pounding in his chest. Henry's mom wouldn't let him play these songs in the house. They were too loud, too vulgar.

His car, however, was his own world—his own little universe. Henry could do whatever he wanted as long as he was driving. It was a 1965 Ford Galaxie, and the leather of the driver's seat squeaked when Henry stepped on the gas.

The car had been a present from his uncle for

his eighteenth birthday at the beginning of summer. Henry's mom had given his uncle a disapproving look when he pulled up in the driveway and honked the horn. She said it was too extravagant. Too fast.

It was the most beautiful thing Henry had ever seen. If given the choice between screwing Kathy Sterling and driving his new car, Henry would probably choose the car. Although screwing Kathy *in* the car would have to be a close second.

She finally let him do it at the end of summer, parked out by the old, deserted bunkers of the far end of town. He thought about the salty smell of the wind off the water as he unbuttoned her shirt. How she sighed when he kissed her. How strands of her dark hair stuck to her lips . . .

Henry pulled into the school parking lot. Even though he was running a little late, he paused, taking a moment to unclench his hands from the steering wheel and just breathe. He closed his eyes and counted to ten, slowly. He was getting that headache again—the one that felt like a vein above his eye might burst.

The headaches had been getting worse for the past few weeks, and his mom said he probably needed glasses. Henry didn't think so. His vision was just fine. And it just didn't feel like something that doctors could fix. It felt bigger than that—almost like his head was trying to rip itself in half.

Sometimes Henry thought he was living in two worlds at the same time. Even as he got out of the car and walked toward the front doors of the school, Henry could feel that familiar pulling sensation—like his mind was being tugged in two directions at once.

On one side was regular Henry. He would go to school and laugh with his friends. He would sit through class and raise his hand just enough that the teachers would notice, but not enough that he looked like a know-it-all. He would sit with Kathy at lunch, letting his hand rest on her upper thigh. That Henry had it so easy.

The other Henry was quiet most of the time. The other Henry liked to sit back and watch. Right then, for instance, he watched a ghost stagger across the parking lot. The ghost was dragging his left foot and clutching his arm. Blood dripped down his face from an empty right eye socket.

There were a few other students still making their way slowly into the school, so Henry couldn't look at the ghost directly. Instead, he smiled at a guy from the football team, giving him a small wave, while the other Henry (the quiet Henry) sized up the ghost.

It was weak, Henry could tell. He could feel the edges of the ghost and practically taste the way it would crumble. Ghosts tasted like dust.

Henry liked this part—dismantling the ghosts. He was good at it. Better than football, or geometry, or even kissing Kathy Sterling. His uncle said he was a natural, though Richard had said it in a grudging kind of way. And Henry was getting stronger every day. Sometimes he wished that he could tell Kathy about the ghosts—that he could show her that he was more . . .

More than a second-string linebacker. More than a straight-B student. He wished Kathy could see who he really was. That he was special.

Henry kept walking toward the school entrance, but slowed a little. The ghost was getting closer. Henry could smell him—the blood and sweat and the sharp, vinegar scent of fear. They were disgusting, the dead. Mindless things, stuck like a record skipping. Henry didn't know why they came back. It was unnatural. At least, that's what his uncle always said.

The dead man looked at him, and Henry struggled to keep from curling his lip. He maintained the pleasant smile on his face—perfectly normal, if anyone was watching him. There was always someone watching. That was another lesson his uncle had taught him. You couldn't let your guard down for a minute.

Then Henry reached out a hand and quickly laid

it on the ghost's face. The man's blood felt greasy and warm on his fingertips, and his cheek sank in slightly, like bread dough. At his touch, the dead man froze, staring at Henry's fingers. He looked like he wanted to say something, but Henry didn't wait. He locked onto the ghost with his mind and ripped him apart. It was over in a second.

Henry put his hands in the pocket of his coat. His fingers were freezing.

As Henry walked through the front door, a woman brushed past him. She was older than him, but striking. Her pale blond hair was pulled up into a bun, and she wore a gray skirt that tapered just above her calves. She also seemed familiar, though, Henry couldn't place where he might have seen her before. No . . . it wasn't that she looked familiar. She *felt* familiar.

He smiled at her, but she just frowned back and kept walking. Henry felt something like static electricity as her arm brushed past his. The air crackled around them, and Henry's mouth tasted like blood.

Henry watched her back as she disappeared down the crowded hall. That strange, flickering, electric sensation faded once she was gone from sight. He wanted to go to the bathroom and wash out his mouth, but he wanted to see Kathy before his first class.

When he got to his locker, Henry found Kathy waiting for him. Kathy was wearing a bright red sweater and a white skirt whose hem hovered around her knees. She smiled when she saw him and waved.

Kathy wasn't beautiful—at least not the way that the women in the pages of *Sports Illustrated* were beautiful (Henry had two of the swimsuit editions hidden in an old shoe box in the back of his closet). Her nose was a little too big for her face, and she was kind of thick at the waist.

At least, that's what Kathy always said. She was so quick to point out her own flaws—cataloging them like she was reading items from a shopping list. Whenever they walked past a store window or a mirror, Kathy would frown and suck in her stomach. But when she smiled at Henry, he didn't think about her nose. He thought about her bare legs in the backseat of his car. Her soft hands. Her smile.

Henry grinned. "Hey babe," he said, putting his arm over her shoulder, She snuggled up next to him.

"Your hands are so cold," she said. Kathy rubbed his hands with her own like she was trying to start a fire.

"Nah, you're just too hot." He laughed at his own stupid joke and kissed her cheek. She *was* warm—her face flushed, and her lips a deep shade of red. Kathy sometimes reminded him of Snow White from the Disney cartoon, with her dark hair and pale skin.

She took his face in her hands and kissed him full on the mouth. Then Kathy pulled back and looked in his eyes, a puzzled expression crossing her face. She shook her head, smiling. "You taste strange. Like . . . chalk or something. Dirt?"

Henry wiped his mouth. It still felt dry and gritty—like he'd been sucking on gravel.

Henry flushed slightly at the idea of her *tasting* him. But then he made himself smile. "Are you saying I have a dirty mouth?"

Kathy laughed, her smile stretching wide across her face. She kissed him again, this time on the cheek.

"And a dirty mind," she whispered into his ear. Then a flock of girls swept by and absorbed Kathy into their midst. She turned back to Henry and wiggled her fingers to say goodbye.

"Find me at lunch!" Kathy called as her shoes clicked down the hall.

Henry put his jacket in his locker and checked his reflection in the little mirror on the inside of the door. He knew he was good-looking, with his father's dark hair and small, delicate nose. But his eyes—green, fringed with thick lashes—those were his own.

Today, however, Henry looked terrible. The

skin around his eyes seemed too thin, and he could see a startlingly red vein in the white of his left eye. He smiled at his reflection. *Better.* Henry smoothed his slicked-back hair and adjusted the collar of his shirt.

It was important, his uncle always said, that he looked *normal*. That no one saw what was really inside him.

The first bell rang before Henry was close to happy with what he saw in the mirror. His headache was a little better—more of a dull pressure than the sharp pounding like it was on the drive to school. He set his hand against his temple and tried to remember what it felt like to *be* normal. He wasn't sure if he ever knew.

Chapter Three

Lorna's new car wasn't new, and it hardly seemed like a car. With its long, sleek body and tail fins, it felt like a spaceship dreamed up by Jules Verne. It was her father's light blue Chevy Impala, but now he was dead so she might as well drive it.

An impala—a real one—was a delicate antelope that lived on the African plains. The car's namesake had long, graceful legs and eyes that looked like pools of black ink. Lorna had seen pictures in *National Geographic* magazine.

Her father's car, on the other hand, smelled of mold and cigars, and she knew for a fact that a family of mice had taken up residence inside. She had seen a little gray body dart across the dashboard when she pulled out of the driveway. The rodent hadn't even startled her because after sorting through her dad's belongings—dumping most of it into boxes to go straight to the landfill—she had seen so many mice that they practically seemed like pets. Or perhaps little furry guardian angels.

She sucked in her breath as another gray blur skittered across the passenger seat.

The only thing that truly bothered Lorna was the smell of mouse pee. It was so pervasive that it felt as if her lungs were developing a thin, permanent lacquer of urine. So it was mouse pee, mold, and cigar ash. Those were all she had left of her father besides her decades-old memories of him.

Her father always used to sit around in his underwear after he got home from the shipyard, propping up his skinny legs on the coffee table and listening to the radio or reading his ratty detective novels. He drank whisky, though he didn't seem to particularly care what kind. Whatever was cheap, wet, and for a few hours let him forget the permanent ache in his lower back.

Long after Lorna had graduated from Grey Hills High School (first in her class) and went to college as far away as she could, the smell of whiskey was still enough to turn her stomach.

She had lived in New York for so many years that it was easy to forget the way that Grey Hills looked in the morning, with the sun on the water and a curl of fog along the shoreline. The first morning after she returned home, Lorna had to take deep breaths to steady herself. It was so beautiful, it almost made her dizzy.

Lorna had never thought of her town as beautiful when she was a girl. Tiny and insignificant, sure. Claustrophobic, definitely. But never beautiful.

She wasn't sad that her father was dead. At least, not in the way she thought she should be. When her mother died in that car accident almost ten years ago now—just after she graduated from college—Lorna had felt like a part of her heart had turned to smoke, and every time she inhaled her chest burned.

That wasn't how she felt when her father, her last remaining relative, died of a heart attack. Normal people missed their fathers. Normal people would feel more than a strange hollow in the pit their stomach that could have been mistaken for hunger or boredom. But Lorna obviously wasn't normal. She had been waiting for him to die for years.

Not looking forward to it exactly—she wasn't a monster—but she couldn't help but think about his life like a great clock winding down. It was just a matter of time.

Lorna hadn't been back to Grey Hills since her mother died. Every year Lorna thought about coming home for Christmas. She had some money saved. Lorna wasn't rich, but teaching in a New York boarding school paid rather well. Better than watching some rich bitch's children, like she had done all through college. The women had always expected her to act like the rest of the help, skulking about as though she were invisible.

Their husbands, however, always noticed her. After her first and only mistake—screwing a balding ad executive in the broom closet—Lorna had avoided the husbands.

She had regretted it the moment his warm, thick hands were on her stomach, working their way up to her bra-covered breasts. Lorna hadn't felt anything but disgust and had pretended that it was a certain boy in high school who had asked her to homecoming. *Danny Coyle.* She still couldn't think about Danny without a bittersweet pang in her chest.

A farmer's son, Danny's hands had been callused but they were gentle when he pinned a rose on her dress and later kissed her cheek. Nothing improper. Not even when she put her hand on his knee on the drive home. He had been a perfect gentleman. Did country boys still have manners?

Lorna pulled into the school parking lot, wondering at how little it had changed and yet how fully her years at Grey Hills High School had been expunged from the building. She considered herself at sixteen: bony knees and white-blond hair that she curled every morning even though it meant waking up before her father had even started the morning fire. Where had that girl gone?

The school looked the same, however, with high brick walls and tall windows that were warped with age—staring out at the water like some sleepy behemoth.

She parked the Impala next to a blue Ford truck that was rusting in huge, oddly shaped patches. The bed of the truck was covered with hay. Lorna's eyes watered, and she wasn't sure if she was suddenly full of nostalgia for her high school days or if she was about to sneeze. Lorna had horrible hay fever.

As she got out of the car, she saw a crow perched on a small tree. It cocked its head at her and made a rasping sound. When she slammed the car door shut, a small gray blur ran down the tire and onto the lawn.

In a flash, the crow swooped down and grabbed the mouse in its beak. The mouse gave off a long, terrified squeak. As the crow flew away, Lorna could just make out the mouse's tail sticking straight out of the bird's mouth. She had always liked crows.

Walking through the front doors was like stepping back in time, but a weird, alternate version of the past where everyone was scrawnier than she remembered and covered with pimples. Girls hurried past in their knee-length skirts and sweaters—shiny hair swishing back and forth. The boys all looked like sullen twelve-year-olds who had stolen their big brother's clothes. One boy—a good-looking young man with dark hair—smiled at her as she walked by, but she just looked past him.

Even though she rather liked the familiar routine of teaching, the students always made her nervous. Perhaps it was that Lorna didn't truly feel like a grown-up—not the way she had thought she would feel in her thirties. She still felt like a child pretending to be an adult. One of Peter Pan's Lost Boys, perhaps. Lost Girl . . . was that what she was? God, she hoped not.

The teacher's lounge smelled like cigarettes and coffee. Lorna had tried to take up smoking when she first moved to New York, but with the combination of her allergies and rather severe asthma, the smoke had made her cough uncontrollably. The smell always reminded her of those women who paid her to watch their children while they watched her—lighting cigarette after cigarette and lounging in their bathrobes.

Lorna didn't recognize anyone in the room. When she first applied for the teaching position, Lorna had the strange thought that some of her old teachers would still be there. Had it been fifteen years? Sixteen? That was apparently enough time to flush out most, if not all, of the old faces.

A young woman, whose round face unfortunately resembled a withered apple, sat in the back corner smoking. An older man with thick glasses was pouring himself a mug of coffee. He looked up at her and smiled.

"You must be Miss Evans, the new teacher." His voice seemed too loud for the room, and Lorna almost took a step back involuntarily. He held out the mug he'd just poured for himself. "Cup a joe?"

She made herself walk over and take the steaming cup. "Thank you." There were smudges on the rim of the mug, and Lorna wiped it with her sleeve before taking a sip. It tasted burnt.

"I'm Mr. Bishop. English."

"History," Lorna said back, feeling like they were reciting code names. "And I'm not actually entirely new. I went to school here."

"Really?" Mr. Bishop smiled broadly, showing a row of very white teeth. He didn't look old enough to need dentures, but his front teeth didn't quite look natural. They were so large and shiny. "I'm a Grey Hills alum myself. What year?"

Lorna paused, then mumbled into her coffee, "Class of '52." Mr. Bishop might teach English, but he could certainly do enough math to figure out that she was well into her thirties.

That decade had taken Lorna completely by surprise. On her thirtieth birthday, her boyfriend at the time had bought her a cake. She had waited to blow out the candles until huge drips of wax ran down into the frosting—as if she wouldn't really turn thirty until the fire stopped burning.

Lorna had broken up with that boyfriend a few weeks later and went out and slept with a man she met on the subway. She woke up at his apartment—a dingy studio that overlooked an alley—and wondered that she hadn't been murdered in her sleep. She had let herself out before he woke up.

"I'm Class of '39, myself." Mr. Bishop chuckled, though Lorna wasn't exactly sure why. Lorna quickly added up his age in her head. About forty-five. He looked much older. Maybe it was the suit he was wearing—so old fashioned. Or his thinning hair.

Lorna took another sip of the (rather weak in addition to burnt) coffee, then set it down on the counter. "Well, I'd better get to class."

He kept talking. "If I may ask, what are you teaching today? What will those young minds absorb on the first day of school?"

Lorna smiled. She actually liked talking about lesson plans. It made her feel a little more organized—more legitimate. "I suppose you could call it local history, but I like to think of it as a ghost story. I'm going to tell them about the Accident."

The people who grew up in Grey Hills didn't usually stop to specify that they were talking about the 1916 deaths when they said "the Accident." Everyone just knew they meant the explosion. But Lorna figured that with all of the rumors surrounding the mysterious deaths, she could probably surprise the kids with a few facts.

She had originally planned something completely different for her first day. According to the syllabus she had painstakingly devised, today was supposed to start the unit on World War II. However, on the drive over, Lorna found herself thinking about her grandfather. It was almost fifty years, to the day, since he had died. She supposed, at this point, that her grandfather had become a part of history.

Lorna pressed her palm flat against her pocket, where the shard of bone rested. The skin of her palm tingled. Surely his story was worth telling.

Mr. Bishop put a hand over his chest as though in fright. "Chills, madam. I have chills." He smiled at her again, his fake-looking teeth catching the light. "I'm afraid my introduction to eighteenth century poetry will be rather boring by comparison."

The lady with the round face walked over to them, emptying her ashtray in the garbage. "June." She said. Then, before Lorna could wonder if she was talking about her name or the month, she added, "June Koffman. Geometry."

"Nice to meet you," Lorna said, quickly growing bored of her colleagues. She wondered if there was a way to teach classes by correspondence. She could just stay home in her bathrobe and grade essays, then mail them back to school. That sounded about perfect.

Chapter Four

It turned out that the frowning woman in the hall was the new history teacher. Henry wasn't sure how old she was, but she didn't appear to be that much older than his classmates. She was short and very slim. With her blond hair twisted up in a tight bun, and skinny arms, she looked like someone playing dress-up in her mother's clothes.

Her face might have been pretty, but her mouth seemed to naturally turn down at the edges and her dark eyes darted around the room like they belonged to a twitchy rabbit. Those eyes landed on Henry, and he sat up a little straighter in his chair.

"Hello class. I am Miss Evans."

"Hello, Miss Evans," the class parroted back. Henry's attention was already starting to drift toward the window, where it overlooked the parking lot and then out to the water. Henry could almost see where the ghost had dragged its useless leg across the pavement.

There were more ghosts than usual lately, Henry had noticed. The man was the third ghost he had seen in a week. Henry normally saw only one every few months, if that. He'd have to ask his uncle about it. Uncle Richard always knew more than he told Henry.

And he lies, the voice in the back of Henry's mind whispered. *Richard lies about everything*. Henry tried to ignore the voice in his head. It made him uncomfortable.

Henry wondered briefly who the ghost in the parking lot had been when he was alive. It was easier to just not think about it. Ghosts weren't really the same people, after all.

Once you died, his uncle had taught him, you

can't actually come back. What people called ghosts were just imprints left on the earth. An aftertaste, once you were done with a meal; the line of dark sand after the tide had already receded.

You should never confuse a ghost with the person it used to be, Uncle Richard told him time and again. *They are not the same.*

Henry sometimes wondered if the ghosts knew who they had been when they were alive. Did they still have those memories? Henry hoped not. He didn't like to think about what might have happened to his dad after he died. The image of his father's shoes swinging in the air in the middle of the dining room came unbidden to Henry's mind. He pressed his thumb nail into the knuckle of this other hand. Pain, his uncle had shown him time and again, was powerful.

The memory of his father faded.

Miss Evans spoke. "I don't feel like teaching history today."

Henry grudgingly ripped his gaze away from

the window and stared at his teacher. Miss Evans leaned against her desk, folding her arms over her sweater. She smiled a strange half-smile and crossed her slender legs at the ankles. The class laughed nervously.

"I think," she continued, giving the class that coy smile again, "that I'd rather tell a ghost story."

Henry tried to swallow, but his saliva caught in his throat. He started coughing, his face turning red. Miss Evans looked at him again—her frown returning.

"Mr. Grey? Are you quite all right?" She stood up straight again, smoothing her skirt with her small hands.

"Sorry. Fine." Henry cleared his throat one last time and then slouched back down into his chair. He wasn't exactly sure why, but he had the distinct impression that his teacher disapproved of him. Not his coughing, not his posture, but him—Henry Grey. It felt like she had taken stock of his whole life and found him wanting. What was wrong with her? Everyone loved Henry. The only other person who looked at him like that was his uncle.

"Well, if you aren't dying, perhaps I can tell my story?"

He nodded, wishing that he was back in bed. He had slept until noon almost every day during the summer, even though his mother had wanted him to go find a job. It wasn't as though they needed the money. His mother just didn't seem to understand that he already had a job—one that stripped almost every ounce of energy from him. Henry was his uncle's apprentice. Someday he would know everything his uncle knew and be just as powerful.

More powerful, that little voice whispered. *Much more.* Henry rubbed his temple until the voice faded.

Miss Evans cleared her own throat and began her story, "Do you all know what happened here, almost fifty years ago to the day?" She seemed to wait for the class to nod along before continuing.

"You must know that this school was built in the early 1900s. In 1917 to be exact. But they actually started construction the year before. They laid the foundation and were just starting to build the school itself. Something went terribly wrong. An accident."

The teacher paused, and the class began to murmur. *The Accident,* Henry could hear them saying. Didn't Miss Evans realize that everyone already knew about that?

"It was sunny, I've been told, the day eleven men died," she went on. "A beautiful day, just like this one. The men could probably see the water shining in the distance while they started their work. The school they were building was just starting to take shape. Some of the men had children who would one day attend the school. They were proud of what they were doing."

She paused and cleared her throat again. Was she actually getting choked up about people who died fifty years ago? Henry was almost embarrassed for her and avoided looking directly at her face. He stared at her shadow instead, where it flared up along the bottom edge of the blackboard.

Miss Evans went on. "What happened that day was a mystery at the time. Eleven men went to work up on the bluffs—right where you are sitting now. Just before noon, there was a huge explosion. Mothers put down their babes and went to the window to see a bright flame burning in the distance. Sailors glanced up from the rigging and saw what looked like a second sun rising on the bluffs. Store owners said their windows rattled and their open doors slammed shut. They didn't know what had happened at first. One merchant who gave an account of the day said it was as though the fist of God had reached down and struck the bones of the new school."

Miss Evans's voice trailed off. She hooked her thumb into the pocket of her skirt and stared thoughtfully out at the class. The teacher didn't speak again for long enough that Henry started to squirm in his chair. He never knew what to do with silence.

Henry watched the edge of her shadow waver as she shifted her weight from one leg to another. Was she waiting for someone to ask a question? He raised his hand.

"Yes, Mr. Grey?" Henry thought she'd be pleased that he was participating, but the tone of her voice was definitely annoyed. And was she actually frowning at him again?

"It was . . . I mean. My uncle told me that it was the welder's fault. That he caused the Accident. Is that right?" Henry's face flushed. He hardly recognized the stammering, stupid voice as his own.

"Your uncle?" Miss Evans raised a single eyebrow. "You mean Principal Grey?"

"Yes. He said that the Accident wasn't a mystery at all. That it was just a stupid mistake."

"Oh, so he teaches history as well?" Her voice

was dripping with sarcasm, and the class tittered with laughter.

Henry didn't say another word. He had no idea what to say to a teacher who was determined to dislike him. He wanted to glare at her, but instead he looked down at his hands, where they were clenched into a tight ball on the lid of the desk. Miss Evans wasn't a teacher. She was something poisonous and scaly.

"Principal Grey is right. It was most likely a welding accident. But no one really knows what happened that day. All of the witnesses are dead. Historians do know that the explosion was consistent with an acetylene-fueled ignition. However," Miss Evan's voice took on a harsher edge, "that does not mean that it was the welder's fault. He had no idea that there was anything wrong with the tank. He would *never* have put his fellow workers in danger. He would never—"

For a moment, while Miss Evans was talking, Henry thought he saw something just over her shoulder. It looked like a second shadow cast across the blackboard, but it was the wrong angle.

Henry squinted at the shadow, making his eyes water. His head begin to ache again. The shadow reminded him of something—less a memory than a physical sensation, like a scent or a taste in the back of his mouth. The almost-taste lingered on his tongue. It was bitter, and dark.

He remembered the strange, electric crackling when he first saw Miss Evans in the hall and the taste of blood in his mouth. Henry glanced down at his hands, and the hair on his knuckles was standing on end.

Henry looked back at the teacher. The second shadow had vanished. He began to doubt that he had seen anything there in the first place.

Miss Evans, whose voice had become a little shrill during her speech, abruptly stopped talking. She had a slightly confused look on her face. "I'm sorry, I think we've been off topic enough for the day. Please take out your books and turn to page fifteen. Now, who can tell me one of the factors that caused the start of World War II?"

As Henry opened his book, a page slid across the pad of his thumb, slicing it. The cut stung and was deep enough that, for a moment, it didn't even bleed. As he watched a line of blood fill the wound, Henry realized that—for the first time in days—his headache was completely gone.

Chapter Five

Somehow, Lorna fell asleep at her desk.

All day she had felt the creeping sensation that she was being watched. Even during her fourth period prep time, when she didn't have any students, Lorna's skin prickled as though a person were standing right behind her, staring at the back of her neck. She kept looking over her shoulder and touching the base of her skull with her fingertips. It felt exactly as if spiders were crawling there.

After the final bell rang and the last student filed out of her room, Lorna was exhausted. She couldn't actually remember the last time, since moving back to Grey Hills, that she had gotten a full night's sleep. Lorna had leaned back in her creaky wooden chair, crossed her arms over her chest, and was just going to close her eyes for a moment. Just ten minutes at the most, before driving back to her father's house.

Her house, she reminded herself once again.

Lorna had decided to sort through her father's books that evening—weeding out the barely read classics (mainly gifts from Lorna) from the yellowed detective novels. They all smelled like the rest of the house—smoke and mildew—but she particularly hated those disgusting books her father had loved, with their lurid stories and illustrations of half-naked women on the cover.

She could just picture her father alone in the house, smoking a cigar and eating a TV dinner, imagining himself to be a crime-fighting hero while his house rotted around him. It was overwhelming when she considered that it was now *her* rotting house, and *her* mildewy, smoky books. All *her* responsibility.

When Lorna jolted awake in the dark, she didn't realize at first that she had been asleep or remember where she was. The residue of whatever dream she'd been having was still thick on her limbs and her heart was pounding.

The dream itself had fled, but Lorna vaguely remembered running from something. Or toward something. She just knew that she had to run, and keep running, or else something terrible would happen.

Lorna often had dreams like that—end of the world dreams. The Russians had finally dropped the bomb or maybe a great tidal wave was about to sweep over Grey Hills.

Even when she lived in New York her dreams had been in Grey Hills. In those dreams Lorna had to reach a bunker or run up an endless set of stairs or maybe dig a hole deep in the ground with her bare hands. There was always something she could do, if she was fast enough. She could save everyone, if only she wasn't so goddamned slow.

This dream, however, felt different—more real, but also less. Like a memory that she couldn't quite hold onto: an acrid scent; the wisp of the color orange. Something bright and hot, but too fleeting to catch. Nothing solid.

Lorna tried to see what time it was on her watch, but it was too dark. Someone must have turned off all the lights without checking to see if anyone was still in the school. She was at once enormously annoyed with whomever had failed to spot her sleeping in the classroom and happy that no one had seen her.

Standing up, she winced as her back made a series of popping sounds. She had a terrible crick in her neck, and her mouth must have fallen open while she slept because the roof of her mouth was dry. There was also a line of saliva on her chin. *Lovely.* Once again, she was grateful that there were apparently no witnesses.

After gathering up her books—feeling for them in the dim light from the windows—Lorna stepped out into the hallway. She remembered, when she was a teenager, wondering what it would be like to see the school late at night, after all the teachers had gone home. *It's dark,* Lorna told her younger self, *and still smells like an old, musty building.*

Lorna was about to walk out the front door to her car when she noticed that there was one light still on. A thin, yellow line shone at the bottom of the door to Principal Grey's office.

When Lorna had applied for the teaching position all those months ago—just after her father died, and she inherited his house in Grey Hills—she had a brief phone interview with Principal Grey. Lorna had remembered him from when she was still a student there. He wasn't the principal then, but a chemistry teacher.

Mr. Grey was so handsome. When he demonstrated what happened when you dropped a sliver of sodium into water, it had burned a bright orange and filled the glass beaker with sparks. It looked like the Fourth of July.

He had sounded different than she remembered when they spoke on the phone. His voice was deep and a little raspy—like tree roots, scraping free of the earth. A smoker's voice.

Lorna could hear Principal Grey speaking, muffled, through the door to his office. There was also another, slightly higher voice. Lorna had always been a curious person and she had the strong urge to press her ear against the wooden door and try to hear what they were saying. But she didn't want to be caught snooping on the first day of school. Or on any day, for that matter. Lorna walked past Richard Grey's office and pushed on the front door.

It was locked.

Lorna rattled the handle and pulled it back and forth, hoping it was just stuck. She even hit the door with her shoulder, as though her one hundred and fifteen pounds could possibly force a locked door to open. She sighed, then turned and walked back to Principal Grey's office.

She could still hear his voice rumbling from behind the door. Even though Richard Grey had hired Lorna himself, she had yet to see him face to face. She had actually expected a follow up interview, or some kind of training before school started, but Principal Grey had forgone all of that. He had inspected her resume, offered her the position over the phone, and told her to show up on the first day of school with a lesson plan.

It wasn't that Lorna was underprepared for the position—she had been teaching for more than a decade, and was always very thorough when planning a curriculum. The whole process, however, had left her with the unsettling feeling that steps had been skipped.

Perhaps she had not been hired after all, a tiny, nearly incalculably small portion of her brain cautioned.

Lorna remembered Mr. Grey as a tall man, with dark hair that was just starting to turn gray at the temples. He couldn't have been much older than Lorna was now, she realized, when he was her teacher. Maybe thirty-six or thirty-seven when Lorna was a senior in high school.

All of the girls had a crush on him, so her small infatuation (with his arms when he rolled up his sleeves during an experiment; with his lips when he was explaining the hierarchy of elements) was quite run of the mill. But about fifteen years had passed since she last saw him. He was probably fat now. Or bald.

Lorna knocked on his office door, her face burning. She felt like a child who had locked herself out of her own house. There was a scraping sound— probably his chair—and then footsteps.

She had missed dinner, and her stomach made an unpleasant grumbling sound. Lorna wanted to disappear, but she wouldn't let him know that she was embarrassed. If nothing else, Lorna always appeared perfectly at ease in every situation. Her face was a mask that she put on every morning.

That is what she decided, years ago, when she first moved to New York, and was so very out of her depth. For the thousand things she couldn't control in her life, she could at least control her expression.

The man who opened the door looked like an older, more handsome version of the Mr. Grey she remembered. His hair was almost completely silver, but he was still very trim.

"Oh." Principal Grey's brows furrowed in puzzlement. "May I help you?"

Lorna extended her hand. She'd found that a hearty handshake was a good way to diffuse almost any awkward social situation. "I'm Lorna Evans. History."

"Of course." He took her hand in his firm grip. "I hope your first day went smoothly. But, may I ask," Principal Grey released her hand, and ran his own through his hair, "what keeps you so late?"

Lorna considered making up an excuse. Maybe she had been grading papers? No—homework wasn't due on the first day of school. After a moment's hesitation, she said, "I fell asleep at my desk, and now I'm locked in."

Principal Grey stared at her for another moment, and then his face broke into a grin. "So you are trapped?"

"Yes." Lorna tried to retain complete composure of her face, but felt a smile tugging at her lips. "Quite."

He laughed, then dug into his pocket and produced a ring of keys. "Well, let's release you, shall we?"

They walked down the hall, their footsteps echoing in the dark.

"You must know," she said, "I don't exactly make a habit of sleeping at my desk."

"Of course," Principal Grey repeated. "But surely someone is looking for you by now? Should I expect a search party banging down my doors? Accusations of kidnapping?"

"Oh, no. There's no one to miss me. I just live

by myself." As soon as Lorna said it, she heard how pathetic her words sounded.

He probably thought she was an old spinster, with twenty cats. Or had a pet pig that she dressed up in doll's clothes and pushed in a stroller. She had heard about a woman who did that when she was a child—though Lorna had never actually seen the pig.

"I'll keep that in mind, in case we require any other late nights." His deep voice was teasing, but he must have noticed how Lorna stiffened at his words. "I apologize. I become rather irreverent after dark."

He unlocked the door and pushed it wide open. "Did you drive here?"

She nodded.

"Then allow me to walk you to your car. You never know what could be lurking in the night." He smiled again, and Lorna remembered the little jokes he used to make in class. He was always laughing—whether at himself or the students, Lorna wasn't always certain.

As a teenager, Lorna remembered thinking of her teachers as lesser gods—untouchable and unknowable. But Richard Grey didn't seem like that anymore. He was just a man—a man who liked to smile.

"No. Thank you, though. If I can't brave the dangers of Grey Hills after dark, then how could I possibly endure a class full of teenagers?"

"Very well, Miss Evans. Take care." He reached out and took her hand again, though she had not offered it. "You know, I do remember you. From when you were my student, I mean."

He raised her hand to his lips and kissed the back of her hand. It reminded her of a kiss a medieval knight might bestow upon a lady—tender and chivalrous. And it especially annoyed Lorna that her stomach fluttered.

She took her hand back.

"Goodnight, Principal Grey." She walked through the door and down the steps without looking back.

From behind, she heard him call out, "Good-night, Miss Evans. Sweet dreams."

It wasn't until she was in her father's car, pulling out of the parking spot—her mouth once again full of the smell of mold and mouse urine—that she realized something. She had distinctly heard two voices in Principal Grey's office, but when he opened his door, he was the only one there.

Chapter Six

When Henry was ten years old he found his dad hanging from a light fixture in the dining room. Alexander Grey was wearing his best shoes. The black leather caught the light, and the shoes seemed to shine white as they swung back and forth—almost imperceptibly—as though propelled by the rotation of the earth. Because his dad wasn't moving himself, and the air was so very still.

It had felt, at the time, like all of the oxygen in the room had vanished. Henry's chest caved in on itself, and he couldn't breathe. Henry didn't remember much else about that day. He couldn't, for example, remember his dad's face (which must have been gruesome), or the clothes he was wearing. Henry couldn't even remember how long he had stood there, staring at his dad's feet, which were at almost the exact same height as Henry's eyes.

However, Henry remembered his dad's shoes. One of the laces either had come untied, or was never tied in the first place, and dangled just below the tips of his dad's toes.

His mom never spoke of that day—how she had screamed when she found Henry standing there, looking up at her dead husband. Henry didn't remember his mom cutting his dad down, but he did remember his dad lying on the floor, and his mom pounding on his chest hard enough to crack his ribs.

It was too late. That was something Henry clearly remembered thinking while he watched his mom wail and slam her fists again and again against her husband's unresponsive form. He had known, even then, that nothing could be done.

It was the first time Henry had ever truly understood the concept of time. That it could, literally, run out. It was like in the cartoons where the long, twisting cord of a fuse burned until it reached the dynamite. His dad had blown his life up. All of their lives. It was hard not to hate him.

Henry sometimes wondered why, in all the years since, he had never seen his dad's ghost. What would he do if his dad had come back?

He had so many questions. *Why did you do it? What does it feel like to die?* None of the ghosts Henry had met had ever answered that question. Of course, he had never asked them.

"And then I found another ghost on the way here," Henry told his uncle through a mouthful of cookie. He was in the study at his uncle's house on Tuesday, sitting across the desk from Richard. That was where they always had their lessons.

That last ghost was horrible. A naked guy with

blood running down his wrists. The ghost had been standing in the middle of the road with his eyes closed. Henry didn't know if the ghost even realized that cars were passing right through him.

Henry was driving to his uncle's house after football practice and had pulled over as soon as he saw the man in the road. He walked up to the ghost, more disconcerted by the man's nakedness than by the blood that pooled on the cement beneath his hands.

The ghost had opened his eyes right before Henry reached out and, with the flick of his wrist, dismantled him. Henry wanted to go home and shower—he felt almost sticky with the memory of the ghost's blood. He was also starving after destroying the ghost and felt a little woozy.

Instead of going home, however, Henry got back in the car and drove straight to his uncle's house. Richard hated it when he was late.

Richard frowned. "So, three ghosts?"

"No, I think that makes four. Remember, there

was that one yesterday—in the parking lot?" Henry took another cookie. Greta, Richard's housekeeper, made the best gingersnap cookies. They were probably his favorite snack after taking care of ghosts. There was always a plate of cookies waiting for him on his uncle's desk.

"So, four ghosts in less than a week," Henry said while chewing. "That's not normal, right? I mean, that's crazy!"

Henry leaned back in his chair and looked around his uncle's study. The far window had a view of the garden, but the shrubbery was so overgrown that all Henry could see was a mass of green through the glass.

"No," his uncle said, his voice barely above a whisper. "Not normal." Then he spoke up louder, in his *teaching* voice. "Do you know why there are so many ghosts right now?"

"Of course I don't," Henry tried to keep the frustration out of his voice. "That's why I'm asking you."

"Don't take that tone with me, Henry. Didn't your mother teach you manners? You *do* know why. You just have to think." Richard would never just tell Henry anything during these so-called lessons. Henry was supposed to figure everything out on his own. It was meant to teach him how to think—how to make decisions after Richard was gone someday.

That's not why he doesn't tell you anything, the voice in Henry's head whispered. *He wants to keep you in the dark. He wants you to be weak.*

"I don't know," Henry said. "But it has something to do with the Door, right?"

Richard had told Henry a little about the Door to the Dead, but not enough. More hints than anything. The Door was just one of many things that Richard always said he would explain to Henry when he was "older" and could "understand." Well, Henry was eighteen now. He was old enough to go fight for his country in Vietnam, but still his uncle kept secrets from him.

He lies to you, the voice whispered. *He keeps lying.*

Richard nodded. "The Door is opening."

Henry waited for him to continue, but he didn't. Instead, Richard walked to one of the many rows of books in his study and pulled a large volume off the shelf. He handed it to Henry. "Take a look. Tell me what you see."

Henry opened the book. Inside were pages from a newspaper, all bound together. He leafed through it, marveling at the ink-and-dust scent of the paper. He turned to the first page. It was an article about the Accident. A black-and-white photo showed the blasted remains of the construction site, while a handful of headshots lined the bottom of the page. Pictures of the dead.

"The new teacher told us about the Accident in History yesterday," Henry said, not looking up from the book.

"Did she?" Richard smiled. Henry wasn't sure if he had ever seen his uncle smile quite like that before, with his eyes as well as his mouth. "And what did Miss Evans have to say about it?"

"Not much. Just that it was, you know, an accident. It was weird, actually. She got upset while she was talking. I mentioned that it was the welder's fault—like you told me—and Miss Evans started defending him."

"Well, look at the article." Richard gestured toward the book. "What do you see?"

Henry tried to scan the words, but couldn't make his eyes focus on them. He liked it better when Richard would teach him something useful during their lessons. Like the time he showed him how to build a talisman, or Token as his uncle called it, to bind a ghost.

It had been fascinating to watch his uncle tie a few strands of hair around a knucklebone and then sprinkle it with blood. That was the most powerful combination, Richard had taught him: blood, bone, and hair. Not only can you control the ghost with it, but the ghost itself would grow stronger.

Henry had never tried it, and he wasn't sure he wanted to. Why would he want to control a ghost? He was supposed to destroy them.

He glanced over the page one more time. Obviously Richard saw something—something that should be obvious to Henry. But what was it? He looked over the names of the dead: George Cooper. Jacob Henderson. William Evans—he pointed to the name. "Are they related?"

"Her grandfather. The welder. He was burned up in the explosion. Grim stuff. I heard that they were only able to identify him by the welding goggles that had melted to his skull." Richard took the book from Henry. "Your new teacher comes from old blood. Her family has lived in Grey Hills for generations."

Just like us. Those were the words that his uncle didn't have to say.

Henry had never really been anywhere but Grey Hills, which meant he had always lived in a town that shared his name. How much of his identity depended on this collection of buildings, and the boats that rocked back and forth in the harbor? What could Henry become, if he wasn't a *Grey* from Grey Hills?

That was something Henry wondered every time he got in his new car. What if he just kept driving? What if he didn't come back . . . ?

Henry looked at his watch. It was almost six p.m., but his mother wasn't expecting him home until eight. He should have time to pick up Kathy. He let his mind wander, thinking about the goose bumps on Kathy's arms, and the soft skin of her stomach. Her wide blue eyes.

As if reading his mind, Richard frowned at Henry. "I think you should quit football this year. And stop seeing that girl—what's her name?"

Henry's face flushed. "Kathy. And you told me to join the team. You said I should make more friends."

"I thought you could handle it. I was wrong. There are too many distractions now. You are never going to be able to take my place if you don't focus—if you don't learn everything that I know."

Before he realized that he had even moved, Henry was standing. His hands shook as he gripped the arms of the chair. "I could take your place right now," Henry heard himself say. "I'm already stronger than you could ever be."

Richard moved faster than Henry thought possible. The slap made half of his face throb and left his ears ringing. Henry blinked furiously up at his uncle, but did not speak.

They stared at each other for a long moment—Richard's hand still raised, and Henry fighting the urge to cover his face with his hands.

Finally Richard said, "Your father left you to me. Is this how you want him to see you behave? Like a spoiled brat?"

Henry shook his head, but didn't break his uncle's gaze. He wouldn't be the one to look away first. With his face burning, both from the shame of his uncle chastising him and from the slap, Henry's head felt clear and crisp—like a night sky free from clouds.

Pain always brought Henry's mind into focus. He could see how small his life really was. And how different everything would be once he graduated, when he could finally claim his inheritance. In less than a year, Henry could finally make his own choices for once in his life.

Richard sighed. "I suppose we're done here for today. I want you to take this book with you. Memorize everything. There is a lesson in here." His uncle placed his hand on top of Henry's head, and Henry tried not to flinch away. "You'll need to know these things when I'm gone."

Chapter Seven

The first ghost Henry ever saw was a woman in the Opal theater. He was eleven years old, and she was beautiful like an actress. Dark, shiny hair and lips pursed like a moth's wings. She just appeared one day while Henry was watching a western by himself.

His dad used to take him to the movies every week, but his mom was always too busy. She had started just giving him a few coins on Saturday mornings and letting him watch all the movies he wanted.

A cowboy was riding across a black-and-white Texas vista, and the empty seat beside Henry was suddenly no longer quite so empty. The woman didn't look at Henry, but watched the screen like it was the only thing in the world.

Right away Henry noticed that he could see through her. He didn't, however, notice the gunshot wound on the side of her head that first day because he was sitting on the wrong side. That day he had watched her profile and wondered if he was dreaming.

Henry never told his uncle about the woman in the theater, even after Richard taught him about ghosts, and how to destroy them. Henry never told anyone about her.

After football practice on Wednesday, Henry went to the movies with Kathy. He was supposed to go straight to his uncle's house for a lesson, but when Kathy asked if he wanted to see a movie, Henry had said yes without thinking of the consequences.

That wasn't true. Henry knew that his uncle would be angry. After the slap from the day before, however, Henry didn't want to see Richard. Henry wanted to punish him.

He didn't care what movie was playing, and Kathy wanted to see *Who's Afraid of Virginia Woolf?* He bought two tickets and they went inside. They had gone to the movies for their first date, so there was always something special about walking through those glass doors with his arm around Kathy's waist. Kathy had actually asked him out, on the last day of school the previous year.

Henry and the other football players were hanging out in the commons during lunch, signing yearbooks and talking about summer plans. Henry had no plans. He wasn't going to work in the mill or join a fishing crew for the summer. He was just going to stay in Grey Hills and let his uncle continue to mold him in his image.

Then he saw Kathy smiling at him from across the room. He had smiled back from his perch on

the edge of a table and nodded, as though he needed to give her permission to approach. Like he was
some fucking arrogant prince. But that's what he
was, when he thought about it: the prince of Grey
Hills.

He was going to inherit a kingdom of the dead.

Kathy walked toward him slowly, her yearbook
clutched in front of her chest. A lot of girls had a
crush on Henry. It wasn't bragging to admit it—it
was just a fact. He'd been out with a few girls, going out to the ice cream parlor and then walking
them home. He'd even kissed a few of them. When
one girl put her tongue in his mouth, he'd been
tempted to bite her.

Girls always made him nervous. It was easy to
be the normal Henry at school, where there were
so many eyes on him. So easy to keep up the act
that he was just like everyone else. But when it was
just Henry and a girl, he felt that quiet Henry be-
coming . . . less quiet.

Henry found himself thinking disturbing

thoughts when it was just him and a girl. He started to notice things about girls—the soft, fragile skin on their necks. How breakable their bird-bone wrists really were.

It wasn't like that with Kathy. From the very beginning she was always different.

When Kathy handed Henry her yearbook to sign, he had accidentally dropped it. Instead of getting all prissy about the bent corner of the binding like some girls might have, Kathy just picked the book up and handed it back to him. Then, after he had signed it and given it back to *her*, she laughed at his inscription: *Have a great summer.*

"That's what everyone writes," she had scolded. "Can't you think of something original?" The way Kathy looked at Henry while she teased melted something inside him. It was as if he suddenly recognized her. Like Henry knew her—really knew her—and had just forgotten until that moment.

"What should I write instead?" he asked, reaching to take her yearbook back.

Henry had known Kathy for years, since elementary school. He always had a few classes with her, but hadn't really noticed her. Not as anything more than a backdrop. Now she was front and center.

"Sorry, you lost your chance," she said, hugging the yearbook tight to her chest again. When she started to walk away, Henry jumped down from the table and took her elbow.

"Wait," he said, "You haven't signed mine yet."

While she started to sign his book, Kathy had looked up from beneath her eyelashes. She met his eyes and then kind of nodded to herself, as though deciding something. Then she finished her inscription and handed the yearbook back.

"Have a great summer!" Kathy said in an extra cheerful voice as she walked away.

Henry waited until she was gone before he opened the yearbook to read the message she had scrawled.

Meet me at the Opal. 8 p.m.

The theater smelled like oil, popcorn, and dust. Henry's stomach clenched—he was always hungry. Kathy didn't want any snacks this time (she was dieting again), but Henry bought his usual popcorn, Coke, and two chocolate bars, though he considered buying three. Henry immediately ripped open the foil wrapper and devoured one of the candy bars—barely tasting the milk chocolate—while Kathy wrinkled her nose at him.

"Hungry?" she laughed. Henry nodded, still chewing.

It was the ghost. He had seen another one just after practice. A girl this time. She looked a little younger than Henry.

She was just standing out in the field right behind the gym. Henry couldn't see exactly what was wrong with her at first, but her clothes were all torn, and she looked like she was covered with mud. Then, when he took a step closer, he realized it wasn't mud. It was dried blood. The ghost was drenched from head to toe in it.

The girl didn't look at Henry—not exactly. She stared at something just past him and held up her hands as though she was afraid of something, or someone. Henry took care of her quickly and then went in the locker room to shower and change. He couldn't stop seeing the expression on her face. It wasn't fear . . . it was anger. Someone had ripped her life away from her, and she was furious.

Every time he destroyed a ghost, Henry felt like he was starving for the rest of the day. But he couldn't exactly tell Kathy that part. Add football practice to the equation, and Henry's stomach was a deep, aching cavern. All the time. He could probably eat one of the theater seats.

He followed Kathy into the darkened theater, his feet sinking into the plush red carpet. They were a little late, and the movie had just started. The light from the projector caught the smoke in the air. Although Henry actually hated smoking himself, he liked the smell of the smoke mixed up with the popcorn and the hot scent of the projector. He had probably invented that last scent, though he swore he could actually smell the heat from the bright light and the spinning, looping film.

The theater was fairly crowded, but they found a few seats in the back off to the side. He made sure that there was a chair open to his right. Then he waited.

The movie itself was pretty boring, though Kathy seemed to enjoy it. She didn't even try to take any of his popcorn—her eyes were completely focused on the screen. A drunken Elizabeth Taylor kept yelling at Richard Burton in their living room. Henry hadn't been paying enough attention to learn the characters' names.

Henry tapped his fingers on the arm of his chair and looked around at the back of peoples' heads. Henry wondered if any of them could see ghosts—

if anyone else realized that the world was so much bigger. He doubted it.

His uncle said hardly anyone in the world could see ghosts, at least not the way he and Henry could. Most people could sense ghosts to some extent: a shiver down the back of the neck or a flash of cold air in a heated room. Most people, however, refused to believe in anything that couldn't be seen or held down and examined.

This age of science, his uncle liked to say, *has made people blind.*

Then a cold hand closed over the top of his. Henry shivered, but didn't pull his hand away. That's how it always went, on good days. The ghost would silently appear beside him and sit with him for the duration of the movie. Sometimes she seemed to just watch him while he pretended to watch the movie. There was something familiar about her, after all of these years. She was his secret.

If he paid too much attention to her, she would

vanish. Henry didn't know her name. He'd asked, once, and she just shook her head sadly and disappeared. He never asked again. Henry had never tried to find out on his own who the ghost was when she was alive. He could have gone to the historical society looked up old obituaries. However, since she didn't want him to know, it felt like it would be a betrayal if he went about it behind her back.

It might break the spell that kept her there.

They would whisper, sometimes, if Kathy wasn't with him. He still liked to go to the movies by himself when he could. It was easier that way. He'd ask the ghost a question about the movie—who was that character? What was going to happen? She would whisper back—but quickly, like she didn't want to miss a moment of the movie. He supposed that, over the years, they had developed a sort of friendship.

Since he had started dating Kathy, a small part of him had felt guilty, as though he was being unfaithful to the woman in the theater. It was a stupid idea, he knew, and it had surprised him the first time he had thought it. It was just one of the dark, slimy thoughts that he wished he didn't have. The whispers that came upon him without warning—like his headaches did—and made him feel out of control.

Today, Henry didn't look at the ghost, and simply let her hand rest on his. The cold of her thin hand seeped into his skin, and Henry had to suppress a shiver. He didn't want Kathy to notice.

When Kathy got up to use the ladies room, Henry leaned over and whispered to the ghost, "Just two more days." Henry wasn't sure exactly what he was talking about, but it felt like the right thing to say.

Then he frowned. *What was that supposed to mean?* Sometimes Henry said things, or thought things, that he didn't really understand—as though some pages to the script of his life had been jumbled and he was speaking his lines out of order.

His headache, which had almost vanished during the film, began to pound out its familiar beat once again. Henry's stomach growled, but he didn't move his hand to take a bite of popcorn, just in case it startled her.

The ghost removed her hand from his anyway. Her dark eyes met his and she frowned.

"No," she whispered, bringing her hand up to the side of her head. "Not yet." She sometimes touched her head wound, almost absently—as someone might worry a loose tooth with her tongue.

Henry often wondered what the ghost thought of the movies. Did she understand when the characters' outfits and cars kept changing with each passing decade? Did she even know she was dead, and that the world was moving so swiftly past her?

From her clothes, the woman had been dead for at least forty or fifty years—though Henry was no expert. His uncle would have probably known just from looking at how she was dressed, but Henry would never tell his uncle about her. This ghost, and this movie theater, belonged to Henry.

He stopped talking to the ghost once Kathy returned, but the ghost still faded away long before the end of the movie. She had probably already seen it before many times, so she surely knew how it would end. He wondered, sometimes, where the ghost went when she wasn't in the main theater. Did ghosts even exist when he couldn't see them? Was it like sleeping to them? Could they just stop *being* for hours at a time?

Henry wondered what it would be like to stop existing. All he could picture was a black, inky sleep that went on and on for all eternity. Henry thought about that Shakespeare quote: "In that sleep of death . . . " But he didn't really think death was like sleep. He hoped it wasn't, because he had terrible dreams.

Henry's headache was suddenly so bad that he started to feel sick to his stomach. He covered his eyes against the flickering light of the screen.

He felt Kathy's warm hand on the back of his neck. "Are you okay?" she whispered.

"Just . . . my head." Henry dropped his hand from his face and took another sip of his Coke. All of the ice had melted, and his hand came away slick with condensation. He pressed the cool palm of his hand to his forehead and closed his eyes again.

Kathy rubbed his shoulder. "Do you want to go?" she said, still whispering. "We don't need to stay till the end."

He nodded. Henry had never told Kathy about his headaches, but she must have noticed by now. There had been days over the summer when he had to cancel a date because all he could do was lay down in the dark of his room with a cold cloth over his head.

It would all end in two days, anyway, Henry thought as they left the theater and got into his black car. Though, for the life of him, he didn't know what exactly those words meant either.

Chapter Eight

"Do you believe in ghosts?" Richard asked, leaning against Lorna's front door. He had walked her home after their coffee date led to dinner and then ice cream at the little soda shop down on Main.

Lorna was so full that the waist of her skirt dug into her stomach. She had to have all of her clothes taken in just before the start of school because she had lost about ten pounds since moving back to her father's house. If she kept seeing Richard, she might need to have them let out again.

Lorna considered his question. Richard had been asking her strange, apropos-of-nothing questions all evening. *Did she believe in good and evil?*

What were her parents like? Her grandparents? Lorna found she liked it. Their date had felt a bit like the conversations she used to have in college that seemed to last all night.

"Metaphorically?" she finally answered. "Or do you mean real ghosts? Like Casper?"

Richard smiled down at her—he really was quite handsome, with his square jaw and dark eyebrows. "Either one."

She had been surprised Tuesday morning, when Principal Grey greeted her in the hallway and pressed a key into her hand. "In case you doze off again," he had said, smiling. The way he looked at her, as he handed her the school key, had felt a little too intimate—as though he were giving her the keys to his own house. When he asked her to have a late coffee with him the next day, Lorna knew exactly where it would lead and how unprofessional it all was.

She said yes.

"Well, I can't say I've ever seen a ghost, but I

suppose I do believe that people can be haunted. Not necessarily by the dead, but by the choices they've made. Haunted by regret. By mistakes." Lorna thought of her father. "Haunted by mistakes other people have made. I think the past sometimes gets ahold of you and won't let go. So yes, I think ghosts can exist, in the 'Ghost of Christmas Past' sort of way. What about you?"

Richard stood up straight. The sun was just beginning to set, and the air felt heavy—somewhere in between the warmth of the afternoon and the cold of dusk. Goosebumps prickled on Lorna's arms. In the amber light, all of the lines seemed to vanish from Richard's face.

"Yes, I certainly believe in mistakes," Richard said, not exactly answering Lorna's question. He reached out and took Lorna's hand. Lorna began to shiver and pressed her lips together to keep her teeth from chattering. "But when, lovely Miss Evans, have you ever made a mistake?"

Lorna could picture the many regrets of her

life like they were a tapestry woven onto her skin. *Danny Coyle, the farmer's son—how she had never kissed him. Most of the men she'd slept with in New York City, but not quite all. Her mother.* But she just smiled and said, "Oh, never, I'm sure."

He grinned and raised her hand to his lips. Richard Grey looked a bit like a wolf when he smiled, Lorna realized. His teeth were so white and slightly pointed. "Would you like to?" he asked, pulling her towards him.

While they lay in her narrow bed later that night, Richard whispered into Lorna's ear. "There are ghosts," he said, brushing her loose hair from her bare shoulder. "I've seen them."

"Real ghosts?" Lorna asked, smiling up into the dark. The night no longer felt real. She was floating and hardly even knew what words were coming out of her mouth. "What do they look like?"

Richard turned Lorna until she was facing him. When he spoke again, his face was inches from hers. "Like us, Miss Evans. They look just like us."

Lorna thought Richard was done talking, but then he said, "Did you know that a person can be possessed by a ghost?"

Lorna shook her head. "Do you mean demonic possession?" It was hard to tell if he was being serious. She hoped not, because they were having such a lovely time. It would be just her luck if the guy she took home turned out to be a little crazy.

"A similar idea, I suppose. Though I've never met a demon. It is more subtle, with ghosts. The saddest part is that a person doesn't even know if there is a ghost inside him until it is too late."

"Are you trying to tell me that there is a ghost inside you? Are you possessed?" Lorna tried to keep a teasing tone to her voice—Richard's voice was so very serious that it was starting to make her uneasy.

Richard chuckled. "What I must sound like to

you . . . but I feel like I can talk to you. I think you of all people will understand what I'm trying to say."

"Me?" Lorna asked.

"You're special, Lorna. Your family was special too, did you know that?"

She shook her head. "I promise you that my family was the opposite of *special*. My father . . . " she paused, her throat tightening. "He was a very ordinary man. Too ordinary. I think he may have died of it."

"Believe me, you have extraordinary blood in your veins. Did you know that the Evans and the Greys have known each other for generations? I think my father was friends with your grand-father."

Lorna thought about her grandfather's ashes on the kitchen counter. She almost mentioned it to Richard, but she didn't want him to think she was morbid.

Then Richard said, "I heard that you talked

about the Accident to my nephew's class the other day. What possessed you . . . I mean, why did you decide to tell them about that horrible day?"

Lorna frowned. It was so dark that she could hardly see his face, but she thought Richard was smiling. "I don't know," she said. "I suppose it had to do with the anniversary coming up on Friday. I thought it would be good to honor the men who died, even in a small way."

Richard pulled her closer, so her head was tucked close to his chest. "Your grandfather would be proud," he said softly, "to know you are carrying on his legacy. You are making Grey Hills a better place."

"Thank you," Lorna whispered. She was so tired that she didn't even try to keep her eyes open any more. Richard kept talking, but his voice was soon just a low rumble in his chest.

While she drifted off to sleep, Lorna couldn't tell if she was hearing his heartbeat in her ears, or if it was her own.

Chapter Nine

When Henry got home from the movie the house smelled like roasted chicken. He dropped his book bag in the front hallway, and went to the kitchen. That's where he found his mother. She was drinking a glass of red wine and singing along to a Patsy Cline record. Some swoony song about walking at night.

"Hi, Mom," Henry said. He took a juice glass out of the cupboard and poured himself some of her wine. His hands shook as he brought the glass to his lips. He hadn't noticed before, but he was freezing.

His mom frowned, still half-swaying to the music, but didn't stop him. The bottle was more than half empty already. Henry wondered what time his mother had started drinking.

"Did your uncle finally let you come home?" she asked.

Henry took a large drink from his glass, then said, "Yeah."

He didn't tell her that he had skipped his lessons with Richard and gone to the movies instead. She would just get mad. Besides, Richard had probably already called and told her that he had gone AWOL today. His mother was probably just waiting to see what excuse he would come up with—trying to trap him in a lie.

He knew his mother didn't like his uncle. After his dad killed himself, Henry's uncle had invited them both to come live with him in the big house. It was the house that Richard and Henry's dad had grown up in, and Richard, being the older son, had inherited.

Henry's mother had refused and stubbornly (according to Richard) kept them in the bright yellow house that overlooked the water. Alexander had left his wife with enough of the Grey family money to do whatever the hell she wanted.

At the time, Henry had been bitterly disappointed that they couldn't go live in his uncle's mansion. It was a big, creaky, old building that seemed to have more rooms than doors. Henry always imagined that there were secret passageways and hidden staircases. He used to go over and play there when he was much younger, before Richard's wife moved out and took their children with her.

Henry and his cousins would hide in the deep closets that seemed to go back into the very bones of the old house. They would chase each other up and down the servants' staircase, popping out of doors that looked like part of the wall. To actually live there would have been the height of any young boy's imagination.

Years later, Henry was glad that they had stayed in his childhood home. Especially now, when he was on the verge of leaving. He would have missed the familiarity of it—how he could close his eyes and recreate each room perfectly, like a movie playing inside his head. Henry could still picture his father sitting in the living room reading a newspaper or opening the front door when he came home from the office.

Henry didn't know what the next year would hold for him. Would he go to college? Would he be drafted and travel halfway around the world to Vietnam? Some of his teammates talked about signing up before they were drafted. Others whispered about going north to Canada, but Henry didn't think they were really serious. Henry knew he wouldn't run if his number was chosen. He didn't think he'd be afraid to fight.

Sometimes, though, he thought about the ghosts that must linger on a battlefield. How many dead soldiers remained once the fighting finally stopped? Would there be a second war for Henry to fight? One that only he could see?

Uncle Richard had fought in World War II, but he never talked about it. Had his uncle also had to fight German ghosts that were still carrying their guns? Could a ghost shoot you?

Henry didn't like to think about that—about what it would mean if not even death could bring peace. Did the ghosts just think they were fighting a war that would never end?

Henry had missed dinner, but his mother had kept a plate warm in the oven.

"It is much too late for a school night," she said, setting the plate in front of him. Henry wasn't sure what time it was; he wasn't wearing his watch. But it couldn't be that late, could it? He had come straight home after dropping Kathy off at her house. Where was his watch? He must have forgotten to put it back on after practice.

His mom walked over and turned off the record before sitting across from him at the table. Even though Henry didn't especially like his mother's music, he would have preferred anything to the scrape of his silverware on the plate and the ticking of the grandfather clock behind the table. It was almost as if the house was trying speaking for them. Filling in the conversations they couldn't manage themselves.

Henry wanted to bring up Friday and what that date meant, but he wasn't sure how. It wasn't that he thought that his mother had forgotten, but actually saying the words seemed hurtful. He didn't want to see his mother's face crumple and then watch her try to arrange her expression into something less broken.

When Henry was cleaning up the dishes after dinner, his mother finally brought it up. "Eight years on Friday. Can you believe it?"

"Yeah," Henry said, scrubbing a pan with a sponge. The hot water was soothing on his cold hands, and the suds sloshed back and forth in a pleasant sort of way. A cut on the back of his hand, however, stung when he submerged it in the soapy water. He didn't remember when he had hurt himself.

"'Yeah?' Is that all you can say? Do you even remember your father?" Sheila Grey used to be beautiful. She was tall, for a woman—Henry had only just reached her height this year. It was strange, after nearly two decades of looking up to his mother, to finally meet her gaze eye to eye. Her eyes were a dark, vivid brown—like syrup, or a burnt honey.

It wasn't that her beauty had faded exactly, but when Henry looked at her now he didn't see the woman from her black-and-white wedding pictures—all youthful glow and soft features. She was somehow beyond beauty. Instead, she possessed the hard, sharp face of a survivor. His mother reminded him of the driftwood that piled up at the high tide line. Utterly changed from the tree it once was, but still there. Still strong.

Henry didn't answer his mother at first. *Did he remember his father?* What kind of a question was that? He wanted to pick up one of the glasses from the drying rack and throw it against the wall. He wanted his reply to shatter and cut. Instead he sank his hands to the bottom of the sink and pressed them there.

"I remember him." Henry said at last. Then, because he knew his mother would hate it, he added, "He looked like Richard."

"Your father would have been ashamed of you." Her whisper would have been barely audible had she not been standing right behind him, her mouth inches from his ear.

Henry didn't know why they couldn't be in the same room without picking at each other like jackals chewing on a pile of bones. His mother knew what Richard was teaching him. But she would never quite forgive Henry for it—for just being what he was. A Seer, like his father before him. Like Richard.

He could see ghosts, and she couldn't. And she blamed Henry for all of it. For his father's death. For the fact that Henry would never just be *normal*.

Hidden beneath the dirty, soapy water, Henry's

fingers touched the edge of a carving knife. For a moment, his hands didn't even feel like his own hands. He pulled them away from the knife, closing his fingers into a fist because otherwise he was afraid he might have grabbed the handle of the knife.

He bit the inside of his cheek because his head had begun to ache again and for some reason that seemed to help. When his cheek started to bleed, his head stopped hurting.

"Eight years," his mother repeated. She took several steps back and picked up her wine glass, refilling it with another splash of red. "Eight years and you're all I have left of him."

"Me and Richard," Henry whispered, turning his head to watch her drain the glass.

As his mother left the room, he thought he heard her say the word "monsters." But he supposed it could have been anything. She was walking so quickly.

Chapter Ten

Richard was gone when Lorna woke the next morning. She scanned her bed for a trace of him—some sign that she had actually spent the night with the astonishing Richard Grey—but didn't find so much as a silver hair on her grandmother's quilt.

When she pushed herself up from the bed, Lorna winced at a sudden pain. On the underside of her wrist was a thin line of dried blood. It wasn't a deep cut, but it stung when she pressed her finger to it. Lorna couldn't remember cutting herself last night, but things had gotten a little rough, so she supposed anything was possible.

A wave of emotion that was somewhere between

smugness and deep embarrassment washed through Lorna. She would see him today, and the next day, and the next. Had it been a mistake after all? *Yes. Probably. Maybe.*

It was only five a.m. There was an abundance of time before school started. Lorna knew she wouldn't be able to go back to sleep, so she started some coffee. While she watched it drip, she let herself remember his hands on her legs and how his teeth had grazed her neck.

When she went to get a coffee mug out of the cupboard, Lorna glanced at the cookie jar—her grandfather's makeshift urn—where it still sat on the kitchen counter. She really should have done something about that already. What would she have said if Richard had tried to open it the night before looking for an actual cookie? Probably just told him the whole story, she supposed, minus the part about carrying a piece of her grandfather to school on Monday.

Lorna still wasn't sure what had possessed her

to put the small piece of bone in her pocket. Was this just the first of even more eccentric things she would do, now that she was a thirty-something woman who had moved back to her childhood home? Furthermore, at what age were you no longer considered an independent woman and relegated to spinsterhood? Lorna was afraid she had already passed that year.

As she stared at the cookie jar, waiting for the coffee to finish brewing, Lorna noticed a large smudge of what must have been ash on the side. Lorna walked over and leaned in close. The smudge curved around the body of the jar like a rather large thumbprint. She clearly remembered wiping down the jar after she first cleaned up the horrible mess of ash.

The only time she had opened the lid since had been to drop the fragment of her grandfather's wayward bone shard inside. Even then, she had not touched the ash. At least, she didn't think she had . . . could she really have walked around with traces of her grandfather on her hands and not known it? Lorna made a little choking sound that was something between a gag and a gasp and held her hands out in front of her. Perfectly clean.

She really needed to give the whole house another scouring before she had any more guests over. Lorna just hoped that Richard hadn't noticed the mouse problem or the pervading smell of cigar smoke. Her embarrassment was starting to win out over her smugness by a landslide.

Lorna carried the cookie jar over to the sink and rinsed it clean again. She wondered how much of her grandfather would eventually end up washed out with the dishwater to the Puget Sound. She thought that would be rather nice—to just float out with the tides and mingle with the kelp and the schools of fish.

Maybe she would go scatter her grandfather's ashes one of these weekends, before the weather completely turned. What would she do with him otherwise? Just put Grandpa up on a shelf for the next five or six decades until her ashes joined him in her own dreary urn?

She left her father's car in the driveway and walked the twenty minutes to the high school, enjoying the brisk morning air and the growing light of a day not yet fully formed. *It still needs to rise*, she had thought, *like bread dough. Like my life.*

Lorna walked past the great house she knew belonged to Principal Grey. Richard . . . Surely, they were on a first name basis now.

The house itself was surrounded by a tall, iron fence, and she imagined that the yard inside was perfectly manicured. There was a light on in one of the second-story windows. She stopped and stared up, hoping that no one was looking down at her. It was still quite dark, so she didn't think she had to worry.

Lorna had heard that Richard's wife had left him several years earlier. She wondered if he was often alone in that big house or if some of the women in town kept him company. The thought that she might be just one of a string of women he slept with made her frown down at her shoes. But she couldn't really blame them—these phantom women who now haunted the edges of her mind. She'd certainly been willing.

When Lorna arrived at the school, she saw a car parked on the far side of the lot. It was still fairly dark to see for sure, but the car looked black and quite expensive. She used her new key to unlock the school and stepped inside. The air felt warm in the entryway—warmer than she would have expected. Perhaps the heater had been left on at night? That seemed quite wasteful.

As she walked down the still-dark hall, Lorna rolled up the sleeves on her cardigan and fanned her face. It was actually quite stifling. She might have to open a window.

When she reached her classroom, she nearly gasped in surprise. Henry Grey was sitting at his desk with his head in his hands. He looked like he was sleeping. Lorna paused, wondering if she should wake the boy. She took a step toward him, then hesitated. She could see the bare nape of his neck and the slow rise and fall of his shoulders.

He twitched in his sleep and made a small whimper, reminding Lorna of a puppy. Lorna wondered what he was dreaming. If she were a high school girl, she would have blushed when she placed her hand on his shoulder and gave him a firm but gentle shake. But Lorna was a thirty-three-year-old woman, and it took more than a handsome teenage boy to make her blush. *It took a fifty-four-year-old principal*, she thought wryly.

Henry startled at her touch, and then jerked his head up. For an instant, Henry looked at Lorna with an expression somewhere between confusion and fear. His brows furrowed darkly over his green eyes, and he looked right through Lorna—as though he could see something right behind her. Something horrible.

Then his expression changed so quickly that Lorna could almost have imagined the strange, fearful look. He smiled and stretched out his arms, yawning. "Oh. Hi, Miss Evans. Was I sleeping?"

"Why are you in my classroom? It is five forty-five in the morning." She hoped he wouldn't ask why she had arrived at school so early—as though she had been caught doing something indecent. But why shouldn't she be here? Students had no idea how early a teacher needed to get to class. For all he knew, Lorna arrived at this time every day.

Granted, she had brought along a copy of *Jane Eyre* and was planning to just read for several hours in the sterile calm of the classroom—enjoying every moment before the first students arrived. And, to be honest, she had started to fantasize that Richard might stop by her classroom while she was all alone. But Henry didn't need to know that part.

Henry's gaze still seemed somewhat unfocused—not quite meeting her eyes. Lorna hoped he wasn't on drugs. But she supposed that it was none of her business if he was. She preferred not to get too personally involved in her students' lives.

He stood up, scooting his chair back with a loud scrape. "I have to go meet my uncle. See you later, Miss Evans."

"In two hours, Mr. Grey."

Henry gave her a causal grin, then walked stiffly toward the door, his shoulders slightly hunched. Lorna hoped she was imagining things.

After the strange, cocky boy left, Lorna collapsed into her own chair. It was uncomfortable, but solid. The heat seemed to suddenly dissipate, leaving her shivering in the empty room.

Chapter Eleven

When Henry woke up in the middle of the night on Wednesday, he wasn't actually sure that he was awake. He felt something cold press against his lips, and when he opened his eyes, he found Kathy's face inches from his own. She gave him a huge smile—like she was just so happy to see him that she couldn't hold it inside.

Kathy kissed him again, cutting off the words he was trying to say: *What are you doing here?* Kathy had never been up to his room before, and certainly not in the middle of the night. She climbed under the covers and pressed the full length of her body against his. Everywhere her skin touched his,

Henry felt like he was on fire—she was so cold. Henry pulled her closer, brushing her damp hair out of his eyes.

Kathy was tugging at the waistband of his shorts, and Henry started to pant and shiver at the same time.

Was he dreaming? He must be dreaming.

"Kathy," he finally said, murmuring into her ear. "What are you doing here?"

She bit his earlobe. "Tell me you love me," she whispered.

"I love you." Henry realized that he had never said that to her before. But he was pretty sure that he meant it. Why was she so cold? His teeth chattered while he kissed her neck and his hands shook when he pressed his fingertips into the soft, fleshy skin just above her hips.

This wasn't like the other times—out by the water, in the backseat of his car. Or even earlier that night, when he had kissed Kathy goodbye in front of her parents' house. Kathy had always been so hesitant—even when they both knew she wanted it too. She always made him make the first move, as though it wouldn't be right for her to actually *want* to have sex.

And even when she finally said yes, she wouldn't take off all of her clothes. She didn't want him to see her stomach, she said. She said she was too fat.

Henry soon realized that Kathy was completely naked. He ran his hands along her bare back and felt the ridges of her spine. He moved them both so Kathy was underneath, and she wrapped her legs around his hips. Henry tried not to make a sound—uncomfortably aware that his mother was sleeping a just two doors down from his—but he couldn't help moaning into Kathy's hair.

She smiled up at him—her teeth caught the moonlight. "Tell me you love me," she said again.

Henry was shivering so violently that he almost couldn't say the words. "I love you, Kath. I love you." Now that he was no longer caught up in the moment, the other Henry—the Henry who had been observing this encounter—spoke up. *Why is she here? In your room? Why is she so cold?*

Finally, Henry couldn't lay beside her for another moment. He was freezing. As he sat up, Kathy frowned at him.

"Tell me you love me," she repeated. There was something different about her voice. He had never heard this strange, insistent tone before. She was almost growling. "Tell me you love me," she said again, louder this time. She was going to wake up his mother.

"Quiet," Henry hissed, as the other Henry's anger and impatience surged up from his stomach.

Why was she here? What the hell was she doing here? Henry's head began to ache again, and he felt that familiar pulling sensation, like his vision was being split in two. Two Henrys looking down at Kathy's strange smile.

Kathy sat up, her hair falling across her chest. Her face was all hard lines and shadow in the moonlight. Deep caverns for her eyes.

"Tell me you love me," she said again, and Henry reached out and grabbed her, his fingers digging into the bony curves of her shoulders. He held her at arm's length, and the cold spread up his hands into his arms. Henry felt like he was floating above his body, watching himself shake his girlfriend so hard that her head snapped back and forth. He watched himself slap her across the face.

"Be quiet," he hissed again. Henry wasn't sure what he would have done—it seemed like he was watching a movie and could no more stop his hands than he could have made an actor on the screen stop talking—if Kathy hadn't reached out her hand and shoved it into his chest. His whole world paused: an inhale with no exhale.

Kathy's hand vanished up to her pale wrist, sticking out just below the center of his ribcage.

She was still smiling, but a smile that Henry had never seen before. Kathy's lips were pulled back to reveal the glint of her teeth. It actually looked more like a grimace then a smile.

"You. Love. Me," she said, slowly. With each word, the air seemed to squeeze from his lungs. She must have had her fist wrapped around his heart. He closed his eyes and reached out for her with his mind—with the same reflex that might cause a drowning person to inhale water instead of air.

Henry didn't pause to think about what he was doing, or what it meant. Grasping the claws of his concentration firmly around her body, Henry scattered each particle of Kathy's ghost to the four corners of his room.

It was so easy. As easy as ripping a newspaper in half or pouring water from a glass. One moment Kathy was crushing the life from Henry's body from the inside out, and the next, she was gone.

Henry opened his eyes and slapped his hand over his heart. He took a deep, gulping breath. The skin on his chest was numb, but he could feel the slow, steady beat of his heart vibrate through his body.

The light from the moon puddled over his bed,

and his rumpled sheets seemed to twist and pulse. He held his hands out in front of him. The moonlight made them look different, too. His hand almost looked like they were glowing.

He closed his eyes again. The blood oozed slowly through his veins, and his head swam. *Did that just happen?* That was Henry's first coherent thought, once the cold started to seep from his body, and he could breathe again without a burning panic throbbing in his throat. *Was I dreaming?*

Henry tried to remember what Kathy had looked like in the darkness, but the last image of her face was already fading from his mind. His fingers still tingled where they had traced the outline of her naked body. Other parts of his body remembered her, too. Henry fumbled with his clothes, pulling back on his shorts and straightening his shirt. *Had that just happened?*

When Henry was eleven years old, right after he started to see ghosts, he used to sleepwalk almost every night. His mom would find him all over the house. Sometimes he would be in the library, facing the wall of books—still dead asleep. Other times he would have one hand on the locked front door, as though he were about to set off into the night. His mother would take him by the shoulders and guide him back to bed.

Henry never remembered these excursions and could hardly believe his mother's stories. Then one night he awoke lying facedown at the bottom of the stairs, with blood dripping into his eyes from a nasty cut on his head. He still had the scar on his forehead, just above the hairline.

His mother started locking him inside his room at night after that. She locked him up every night for about two years. She only took off the lock when she discovered that Henry had been pissing out the window when he couldn't get up and use the bathroom and was killing the rose bushes below.

As Henry sat on his bed, still staring wide eyed into the dark of his room, the urgency of the past few minutes started to fade. Maybe it *was* just a dream. Henry picked up the pillow where he had just seen Kathy rest her head. He pressed it to his face and inhaled. Kathy smelled like perfume, and sometimes oranges. The pillow case smelled like nothing—or maybe just his hair gel.

"It was only a dream." Henry said the words out loud, blinking into the shadows. There was something final about hearing his own voice—like a soap bubble popping. "Only a dream," he said again, and sank his fingernails into the skin just above his heart. Even when his nails broke the skin, leaving behind bleeding half-moons, he felt practically nothing.

Chapter Twelve

The first thing Richard had ever taught Henry about ghosts was to not feel sorry for them. The other rules and lessons—how to guard your mind against a ghost; to use a knife until you could use your mind to feel the gritty, sticky substance that held them together and rip it apart—all of these came later. First and foremost, Henry had to understand that ghosts should never be pitied.

They had already had their chance on earth, and feeling sorry for a ghost would not bring the person back to life. The person and the ghost were two separate things. Crying over a dead thing would only make you weak.

As Henry lay awake, trying to decide if what just happened with Kathy had all been a dream, he thought back to the first ghost he was supposed to destroy but couldn't. Henry was twelve years old at the time. He could still picture his uncle standing over the dead girl, the knife in his hand. He looked . . . happy. Like he was enjoying himself.

The ghost was kneeling on the ground, her hands covering her head. She didn't seem to know she was dead—that was the part that Henry couldn't get out of his head, even after all those years. She looked afraid.

The ghost wore a pale blue dress that was already splattered with blood. Before she covered her face, Henry saw a slice down her cheek and dark bruises around her neck. Henry should have just done it himself, but there was something about the girl that made him afraid to try.

He didn't want to mess it up. He didn't want her to be in any more pain.

When his uncle took the knife from Henry's hand and approached the ghost, she had looked right at Richard and put up her hands. His uncle kicked her in the stomach, and she doubled over.

"Like this," Richard had called back to Henry. "Catch them by surprise. That's the best way." Then he jammed his knee into her face. Henry had to look away while his uncle held her by the hair and forced her to her knees.

Ghosts weren't real. They weren't people. It didn't matter how you destroyed them, as long as they were gone. But Henry couldn't forget that smile on his uncle's face when he plunged the knife into the back of the girl's neck as she cowered before him.

"You see," Richard had told Henry, handing him back the knife. "You can't feel sorry for them, or you'll hesitate. If you hesitate, you'll die. Do you want to be dead? Like your father?"

Henry had shaken his head and clutched the knife to his chest. He didn't want to be dead, and he especially didn't want to be like his father. His father was a coward.

When the morning light started to trickle through his window, Henry couldn't lay in bed anymore. He got up—before his mother, even— and drove himself to school. He needed to talk to his uncle.

Henry decided that it was definitely a dream. He had had realistic dreams ever since he could remember. Sometimes he dreamt about a light that was so bright that it melted the skin from his hands. He would wake up with his hands curled into claws, writhing in his sheets. Henry had heard that you couldn't actually experience pain in a dream, but he knew he felt a vivid, scorching pain that was so intense that the only way he could describe it was as white as a star clenched in his fists.

As Henry drove, he inspected the red, angry-looking cut on the top of his hand. He tried again to remember how he had gotten it. The cut almost looked like a cat scratch.

The door was locked, but that didn't bother Henry. His uncle had given him a key a few weeks before school started. In case they needed to meet in his office, Richard had said, though that had seemed unlikely at the time to Henry. They always had their lessons at Richard's house.

His uncle wasn't there yet. Henry probably should have just gone to his uncle's house, but he hadn't really realized how early it was. And who knew how early his uncle got to work. Henry didn't want to wait in Richard's office, so he went to his history class, which he knew would be empty at that time in the morning. Every class should be empty. Something about the classroom just felt right, he thought, as he sat in his desk and stared up at the chalkboard.

As Henry clutched his bag on the desk, waiting for his uncle to arrive, he began to grow tired. His head drooped, and before he knew it, Miss Evans was shaking him awake.

As soon as he opened his eyes, he saw a ghost with dark goggles standing right behind Miss Evans. Henry almost shouted for her to run.

The ghost had placed its hand on her shoulder, though she didn't seem to feel it. Her face, however, looked blotchy, and there were beads of sweat along her scalp, where her hair was pulled back into her usual severe bun.

Henry had never met another person, besides his uncle, who could see ghosts. But that didn't mean that ghosts couldn't see them. He didn't shout, and he didn't warn her. He just smiled and left as soon as he could.

As Henry left the classroom, the ghost followed—exactly what he'd hoped the ghost would do. Sometimes ghosts knew when someone could see them, and it would fascinate them like a cat with a string. Henry could feel the ghost behind him like a wall of flame—the skin on the back of his neck crinkling with the heat. What kind of a ghost gave off heat like that? Kathy had been so cold . . . but that was just a dream, right?

This ghost felt stronger than any Henry had ever felt before. It was almost as if Henry had the ghost on a fishing line and was reeling him in. Henry didn't know what you did, however, once a ghost found its way into your net.

Once Henry had lured the ghost out into the empty hallway, he turned and reached out his hand to touch the ghost's face. He placed his hand on the man's cheek, then jerked his hand back as though burnt. He was burnt, Henry realized. The tips of his fingers had turned an ashen white as if he had just touched the top of a stove.

"Fuck," Henry hissed, and the ghost cocked his head back at him. Henry tried to see through the dark goggles to the man beneath, but he couldn't. They were just black, like the stuff the Indians had used to make arrowheads. *Obsidian*—that was it.

The ghost's face, beneath the goggles, looked

very familiar. Henry was sure he had seen this man before.

He slowly walked to his uncle's office and opened the door with the same key. The office smelled like incense and was chilly until the ghost entered the room. Then it was hot—almost unbearably hot. *What was this ghost?*

Henry reached out his mind again and tried to grab ahold of the ghost—feel him out—but he was too . . . slippery. That was the only way to describe it. Henry sat in his uncle's chair, and the ghost leaned against the wall opposite him. There were flames in the ghost's goggles, and Henry noticed small, black marks forming around the ghost's shoulder—as though the wall itself was starting to burn.

"Who are you?" Henry asked the ghost. He had never met a ghost who could actually hold a true conversation with him, but some, like the woman in the theater, could speak a little. They could answer a few questions.

The ghost smiled. His teeth looked dark, and slick with something. Blood? Henry couldn't tell. The ghost licked his lips, and then made a sound that was something like a deep breath or a sigh.

"Release me," the ghost said. His voice was deep and gravelly, and Henry felt like some nerve deep within his body had been struck and set to vibrate. Where was his uncle?

"Who are you?" Henry asked again. The ghost didn't speak this time, but continued to stare back at Henry. The ghost wore dark coveralls, and they looked like they were charred. Even for work clothes, his coveralls and boots looked old, as though he had stepped out of a picture of the Great Depression or earlier.

Henry tried again to feel the ghost. He concentrated on the man's throat and reached out with an imaginary hand. Henry tried to catch hold of the ghost's trachea and the fragile sinews and veins in the ghost's neck. Sometimes that was the most effective way to subdue a ghost—grab them by the neck.

Once again, it felt like Henry was trying to claw at wet glass. He couldn't find a place to hold on. The ghost smiled at him—a mocking smile, Henry thought—and shook his head.

"Let me go," the ghost said. Henry wanted to cover his ears to block out the echo of the ghost's voice.

They waited like that—Henry's eyes locked on the flat, unblinking goggles of the ghost—until his uncle arrived. Richard opened his office door and frowned at Henry in his chair.

"What are you doing here?" Richard asked.

"Richard." Henry began, still looking across the room to the ghost. "I found something I thought you'd like to see." He tried to keep his voice calm, but he felt like he was slipping off the edge of a cliff he hadn't even known existed until that moment.

"Can you actually see him?" Richard asked, gesturing towards the ghost. "You can, can't you? I can't, isn't that strange? I can feel him though . . .

the heat of him. The power. But I can't see him. What does he look like? Is he covered with burns?"

Henry couldn't take his eyes off the ghost.

"No," Henry managed to say. "I mean, he doesn't look burnt. He looks . . . burning. Everything he touches seems to burn."

The ghost smiled broader, and Henry shuddered. "Can you, you know, take care of him now? It isn't working when I try."

Richard shook his head. "Of course it's not. You're not strong enough."

Henry's head throbbed seemingly in response to Richard's words. *You'll be stronger than him,* the voice in his head whispered. *We'll be stronger.*

"Aren't you going to do something?" Henry managed to say out loud.

Richard didn't answer his question. "Why weren't you at our lesson yesterday?"

"Is that important right now?" Henry watched as the ghost crossed his arms and looked at Richard, as though he was also waiting for the answer.

"It is actually incredibly important. Where were you yesterday?"

"I took Kathy to the movies, okay? Can we deal with this . . . situation now?" Henry didn't like to say the word *ghost* in front of actual ghosts. They didn't always know that they were dead, and it could just make them mad.

For a moment Henry considered telling his uncle about the dream he had last night. Even with the burning ghost staring at him, he was impatient to tell someone . . . to hear his uncle say, *Don't worry, it was just a dream.*

Then Richard crossed the room and took Henry's face in his hand. "I told you that girl was nothing but a distraction."

Richard gestured to the ghost. "If you had come to your lesson yesterday, I would have told you about this ghost. I would have told you about my plans. Our plans. But you couldn't even show up. Is that the kind of Seer you will be when I'm gone? Is that who you want to be?"

Henry had only heard Richard use the word "Seer" a few times. Richard's brother, Henry's father, had been a Seer. Richard was a Seer, too, but not as strong a one as his brother.

Not as strong as you are going to be, the voice whispered again.

"No, sir," Henry managed to say through clenched teeth.

Richard let go of his nephew's face, and then patted his cheek. "You're going to be all right, my boy. I wish it didn't have to be this way. I wish you didn't make me do these things."

What things? Henry wondered as he left his uncle's office and went to go wait for school to start in his car. He saw Kathy's face again, how she looked the night before—full of shadows.

What things does Richard do?

Chapter Thirteen

Thursday went by achingly slow. Lorna found herself on several occasions staring silently at the students, her mind completely empty. It was kind of like forgetting your lines in a play, she imagined. And the students had stared back just as vacantly. They seemed to feel the end of summer like lead poisoning seeping into their blood. Many of the symptoms were the same: irritability, sluggishness, an inability to concentrate.

Lorna sometimes wondered what the point of schools were. Were children really meant to be cooped up all day, hidden away from the sun? Were teachers?

Richard smiled at her when they passed in the hall, but didn't exactly seek her out. Lorna imagined herself slinking into his office and locking the door behind her like she was a Rita Hayworth, instead of tiny, obscure Lorna Evans.

At the end of the day, Lorna walked home and finally went through her father's books. She didn't really sort them, but just dumped them all into an empty box. Her father had written his name into the front page of each one in tidy, square letters. She had considered donating some to the local library, but who would want them if someone else's name was in them?

Among his books she found something interesting. There were a few old newspaper clippings trapped between the pages of an old, musty dictionary. Why her father had placed them there Lorna would never know. Maybe because it was the biggest book he had in the house?

The clippings were old, starting in 1915. There was an article about plans for a new school. The land, the article read, had been generously donated by brothers Kenneth and Eli Grey. Another article mentioned that bones had been found on the land—human bones. They showed signs of having been burnt. The local authorities thought that they were Indian bones, possibly from a funeral pyre. One lurid hypothesis was that the natives had taken part in some kind of ritualistic sacrifice.

Lorna wondered why she had never heard about the bones before. There were so many—at least fifteen individual skeletons had been uncovered. Surely that was worth learning about in history class.

Five other news articles covered plans for the new school up to the time of the Accident. For some reason no one had bothered to keep a clipping about that terrible day.

That was when Lorna thought to look in the front of the dictionary. There, on the inside of the front cover, she read the name "W.C. Evans." So it wasn't her father after all who had kept the clippings. He may have never known that they were there. When did her father look in a dictionary? Her grandfather had probably kept them when he started working on the school. That was why the clippings stopped. He wasn't around to collect them anymore.

Lorna had never exactly grieved for a grandfather she had never known—one who would have surely been dead by now anyway had he not been killed fifty years earlier. But now she swallowed back tears as she sat on the floor, with the clippings that her grandfather had collected with his own hands spread out around her.

If she didn't cry for her own father, then she certainly wouldn't cry for a man she had never met.

Chapter Fourteen

Henry didn't see Kathy at school that day. He went to her parents' house after school, but her mother didn't know where she was. She thought Kathy had come home after they already went to bed, which was very unlike her, and then left before they got up. Her mother was actually waiting to have a "talk" with Kathy. She wanted Henry to have her come straight home if he saw her.

When Henry left Kathy's house he got back in his car and started driving.

It had to have been a dream. It had to be . . . unless it wasn't.

Unless Kathy's naked body was lying dead

somewhere. He tried to remember what Kathy had looked like in the dark. Were there any marks on her? Any sign of how she had been killed? Her skin was so smooth—unmarred by any wounds. He just remembered how cold she had been. But . . . it had to have been a dream, because things like that just didn't happen. People didn't just die like that.

Except, that dark, raspy part of his mind reminded him, *they do. All the time.*

Henry drove to his uncle's house for his lesson because he didn't really know what else to do. He couldn't exactly go to the police and say that he saw Kathy's ghost.

He let himself in and went straight to Richard's study. A plate of chocolate chip cookies was sitting on his uncle's desk. Greta had certainly gone home already, but she always remembered to leave a treat for Henry. Henry was glad that Greta wasn't there. God only knew what his uncle was up to.

Henry didn't have to wait very long before his uncle arrived.

"On time. Good," Richard said, pausing to look into Henry's face. "You look terrible. Have you been sleeping?"

Henry could have said the same about Richard. His uncle had huge bags under his eyes and the lines around his mouth were more severe than usual.

"Actually—" Henry started to say, but Richard cut him off.

"Tomorrow is a big day for us," Richard said. "You read the book I gave you, right?"

"The newspapers? Sure." Henry hadn't actually read them. He had given them a cursory glance, but that was all. He had other things on his mind. Like Kathy. "But I was hoping—"

"Then you know what is happening tomorrow. You understand, right? What I have to do? What *we* have to do?" Richard had pulled out his desk chair but didn't move to sit in it. He was waiting for Henry to speak.

Henry shook his head. "What?"

"The Accident," Richard said slowly, "happened fifty years ago tomorrow. I was hoping you would show some initiative—some imagination—and figure it out on your own. The way your father did. That you would finally show me that you have some of his spirit in you, the kind you'll need to take up the mantle once I'm gone. But I'll spell it out for you. The Accident was a ritual. A sacrifice. The men who died . . . their deaths kept the Door closed for another fifty years. The Door which is now opening."

"Oh," Henry said, but it sounded more like the sound he might make had he just been punched in the stomach. A sacrifice? "Why didn't you tell me this before?"

"Why didn't I tell a child that a Door to Hell was opening, and we needed to perform a ritual to keep it closed?" Richard laughed. "When should I have told you? When you were old enough to drive? When you were old enough to drink?"

Henry shook his head. "You could have told me at any point. You had to wait until now?"

"You didn't need to know before now. I . . . I won't be here forever. I just need to know that you can do it. That you can carry this with you for the next fifty years. That you will perform the next ritual. I need to know that you are capable of this on your own."

"What is the ritual? What are we supposed to do?"

"*We* aren't doing anything . . . not this time. *I'm* doing the ritual this time. But you'll learn." Richard leaned against the desk and didn't look at Henry, but down at his own hands instead. "You will do it next time. In fifty years."

Henry could hear the whispers again, racing and twisting in his skull like rushing water: *he lies, he lies, he lies, he lies.*

Henry returned to his uncle's house after dark and parked three blocks away. Even if his uncle could have seen his car from his window, the pitch-black paint job would have masked it in the shadows. It was almost one in the morning, but Henry didn't feel tired at all. The moon was humming in his blood.

Sometimes, even before Henry saw a ghost, he could taste it in the air. A dusty, iron taste—like a mixture of dirt and blood. It was almost a smell, but filled both his nose and mouth, nearly making him gag. Henry had asked his uncle, once, if Richard could taste ghosts. His uncle just shook his head, with a mystified expression on his face.

"Fascinating!" Richard had said. Henry remembered that clearly. *Fascinating*, like Henry was a science experiment. But no, it turned out,

Richard could not taste ghosts. So there was one more thing that Henry could do better than his uncle.

You're stronger than he is, the voice in his head whispered again. *You were always the strong one. Like your father.*

When Henry pushed open the gate to his uncle's property, it swung open silently. He shut it behind him and walked in the dirt beside the gravel path so his feet wouldn't make a sound. While Richard's wife was still living there, the topiary in the garden had been perfectly pruned and shaped so they looked like wild animals. Henry remembered green lions and hippos and one horse frozen mid-gallop. Now the animals had been allowed to grow out until they were unrecognizable, grasping blobs, and even the grass came in patchy and uneven.

Deep shadows cut across his path and Henry tried to avoid any fallen sticks that might snap underfoot. It wasn't until he quietly walked up the front stairs that he tasted the iron tinge of blood on his tongue. The hair on the back of Henry's neck stood on end, and his stomach tightened. Henry looked all around, but didn't see anything.

Keep going, the voice in his head scolded him. *You have to keep going.*

The door was locked, but Henry had a key. He let himself inside, and then held his breath as he closed the door behind him. For some reason, Henry was suddenly sure that the house was empty. There was a stillness—a perfect calm in the air that made Henry think of abandoned kingdoms and cities overgrown by jungle vines. Forgotten civilizations. But the house always felt empty to some extent, even when his uncle was inside. There were too many rooms. Too much stagnant air in the corners of the house.

The taste of blood still lingered in his mouth and stung his nose. He was started to sweat, even though he knew that the huge, drafty house was cold. Henry began to wonder if Kathy's ghost had broken something inside of him when she grabbed his heart. Had any of that actually happened? Could it have been a dream?

The door to Richard's study was locked, and Henry didn't have the key this time. He rested his head on the wood door and took a deep breath. Then, almost without thinking, Henry took hold of the doorknob and held it in both hands. He heard a crackling sound, like static electricity. His fingers began to tingle.

Henry watched the doorknob begin to glow beneath his hands. He could see the bones of his fingers beneath his illuminated skin. What was happening? Henry knew that this wasn't right— that things don't just start glowing when you touch them. But that part of his mind grew hazy and muted until he could barely even hear himself think. The crackling sound was so loud in his ears.

Then something inside the doorknob made a snapping sound. Henry turned the knob, and the door swung open.

The moon brightened one side of the room in a colorless light. The walls were lined with books, and Henry tried to find the shelf—the one that held the secret compartment.

What? Henry frowned and clutched his head with both hands. Henry had never thought about any "secret compartment" before that instant. *Was he losing his mind?* But he knew—just like he knew the color of the sky or the scent of roses—that his uncle was hiding something. And he knew where to look.

Henry could have turned on a light, but that might have given him away in case his uncle came home. He still wasn't sure why he knew his uncle wasn't in the house.

Trust me, the voice in his head whispered. *I know what I'm doing.*

After running his fingers beneath the lip of several shelves—his shoulder throbbing with the motion—Henry felt a latch. He pressed in on the latch and pulled. The shelf swung out and to the side, revealing a small compartment. There was an old-looking book inside.

A thrill ran through Henry, and he smiled broadly. He felt a sudden rush of pride at the sight of the book—a protectiveness. He remembered the weight of it in his hands. But that didn't make sense. Henry had never seen the book before. He shook his head, trying to make sense of the warring memories in his head.

As he picked up the book—a slim, dusty-smelling volume—Henry felt a cold object against the back of his hand. Something metal. The compartment was deeper than he had thought at first, and he had to stand on his tiptoes to reach all the way to the very back corner. Before Henry closed the compartment, he pulled out two more items. The first was a wooden cigar box with something inside that rattled when he picked it up.

The second was a gun.

Chapter Fifteen

Henry waited to open the wooden box until he was in his car. The gun was safely stowed beneath the books, in the bottom of his bag. He had never fired a gun before, but when he first held it in his hand there was something unmistakably familiar about the heft of it. Henry knew that he could use it, if he needed to.

If Richard makes us, the voice in his head whispered.

When he first left the house and walked into the cold night air, the heat from his uncle's house seemed to follow him. And the box, where he held it clutched beneath his arm, felt heavier than it should be, almost as though something living had been forced into its confines. *A genie in a bottle*, he suddenly thought.

Inside the box, Henry found a few pieces of what he thought at first were shards of broken pottery. He moved them around with his finger and felt that same electric sensation from when he had held the glowing doorknob pulse up his wrist.

Henry shook the shards into the palm of his hand, and holding them up to the dome light in his car, he took a closer look. They were white, with a dusting of rust or dried blood. There were also a few strands of hair that could have been silver or pale blond scattered among the broken pieces.

As Henry poured the shards from one hand to the other—wondering what value his uncle had placed on a broken dish or mug—Henry tasted blood in his mouth again. Then he felt something so hot on the back of his neck that he yelped in surprise and almost spilled the shards onto the floor.

Glancing up to the rearview mirror, Henry saw a man's face in the backseat of his car. It was the man with the dark goggles and a light was flickering in their depths. His hand was raised and hovered just inches from the back of Henry's neck.

Henry almost dropped the shards (bones, he suddenly realized . . . the ghost's bones), but closed his hand around them instead. He whispered, "Stop," in a shaky, hoarse voice. The ghost drew his own hand back and vanished.

He held his closed fist in front of him for a long time—staring in the mirror at the back seat of the car. The ghost didn't return. Finally, when the cool night air displaced the heat that had come from the ghost, Henry lowered his hand and returned the bones to the box.

Fascinating, Henry thought to himself, a smile slowly spreading across his face.

Henry started the car, knowing that he couldn't let his uncle find him there. Then he drove. He didn't return home, but made a wide circle around the town, driving past the theater on Main Street, and then up to the narrow back roads that had no streetlights.

He didn't realize where he was going until he reached the abandoned bunkers. Soldiers used to be stationed there, during World War II, with huge guns meant to protect Puget Sound from enemy ships and submarines. Now it was a park, and people could walk through the long, concrete tunnels and climb up to the battlements where the soldiers, with their cannons and guns, used to stand guard.

This was where Henry had slept with Kathy for the first time—parked where they were hidden from view by the old structures of war. She was worried that Henry was going to be drafted now that he was eighteen and so why should they wait? Why should they wait for their life to begin if everyone was dying?

At the time, Henry certainly wasn't going to argue with Kathy's logic. Now, as he thought back to her words, something heavy filled his chest. What if Kathy's life was already over before it began?

Henry got out of the car and took his book bag with him. There was a path you could walk that wove down to a thin, rocky beach below the bunkers. Kathy had shown him this spot on one of their first dates. She made him a picnic, and he held her arm while she slowly picked her way over the uneven, root-snarled path in her slippery shoes. It was a place that was hidden from view unless you took that slight, twisting path. Their secret.

Kathy had been cold when she crawled into his bed the night before—in the dream that had to have been a dream, but wasn't. Cold, but otherwise untouched. Perfect. After he stepped out of his car and looked up at the giant moon that hovered over the water, he remembered something else. Her hair had been damp.

Henry found her on the beach immediately, almost as if he had known where to look. Naked, she lay half in and half out of the water. In the light of the moon she looked like a statue, or a painting of a person, instead of lifeless flesh and blood.

He pressed his hand to his heart again, remembering how it felt when she plunged her hand into his chest. He wondered what, if any, marks she had left on that fragile muscle.

Leave. Go now. Henry's thoughts cautioned him. *Leave her here.*

Henry walked across the uneven gravel and pulled her out of the water, trying to lift her in his arms. She was too heavy. When he let her go, her body rolled onto the gravel—one arm falling across her face.

Go now! screamed the voice in his head. *Go now and kill Richard for what he's done.*

Henry shook his head. Why would Richard do this? Why on earth would he hurt Kathy?

He didn't want you to see her anymore, said the voice in newly calm tone. *He's a killer. A monster.*

Henry looked up at the moon, because he couldn't look at her body for another moment. What had Henry done when he'd destroyed Kathy's ghost? Had he also destroyed her soul? Was Kathy really gone forever?

After a few moments, Henry opened his bag and pulled out the wooden cigar box. He shook the bones into his hand.

"Pick her up," Henry said, looking out across the water, where the moon's reflection wavered. "Pick her up but don't hurt her. I don't want you to burn her."

Henry didn't know for sure that it would work, but he wasn't exactly surprised when the man with the goggles appeared. More relieved than anything. The ghost lifted Kathy's body, almost tenderly, and walked up the path with Henry following close behind.

After Henry opened the trunk of the car, the ghost set Kathy inside. Then the ghost stood there in silence, as though waiting for Henry to give another command. Henry looked where the man's eyes should have been. It was hard to tell how old the ghost had been when he died.

"How did you die?" Henry asked the man, because he couldn't ask Kathy. The ghost just shook his head and vanished.

Henry thought he might start to cry when he closed the trunk over Kathy's cold body, but he didn't. Was she the sacrifice his uncle was talking about? Part of the ritual to keep the Door closed? Was this what Richard refused to tell him?

Yes, the voice insisted. *Richard lies. He is a liar and a killer.*

As Henry started driving back to town, he suddenly felt calm, knowing that Richard was going to pay for what he'd done.

Henry started to talk to himself as he drove. "What has he done to you? What is he going to do?" Henry wasn't sure if he was talking to Kathy, the ghost with the goggles whose bones were in the cigar box, or himself. Henry's head was foggy. His eyes kept closing, and once he snapped them open only to find the car had almost gone off the road.

Finally, Henry made it home. After parking the car in the driveway, he went inside and dropped his book bag in the front hall—just as he normally would after school. Henry went upstairs and collapsed on his bed. He fell asleep almost instantly.

He dreamed of fire. A crackling, popping, roaring fire that felt like a wall of heat in front of him. Within the dream he knew he had to walk through the fire, but he also knew that the fire would burn him alive.

Henry didn't think about where he was in the dream, but later, when he tried to remember the dream, he figured that it must have been his uncle's house. He held out his hand and felt the heat curl the hair on his knuckles and singe the tips of his fingers. The fire was so loud it almost sounded like a voice talking. A rumbling, haggard voice arguing with itself. Henry took a step forward and felt the toes of his shoes start to smolder.

When Henry woke, he thought the dream was real because he could still smell the smoke. Henry opened his eyes, not sure where he was for a moment. He often woke like that—blinking at the same walls he'd known all his life, but unable to recognize them for a few heartbeats. His mom once told him that, just after his father died, Henry used to wake up screaming.

Henry sat up and reached for the water on his nightstand. He drank and drank, but his mouth still somehow felt dry and sticky at the same time— like he'd been chewing dirt all night.

Smoke. He definitely smelled smoke. Henry swung his legs out of bed.

As he walked barefoot across the hardwood floor, he stubbed his big toe on a broken floorboard. The board was warped and had come loose on one end.

He'd been meaning to dig his dad's old toolbox out of the basement and put a few more nails in it.

Henry forgot, for those few moments, that Kathy was still in the trunk of his car. When he remembered, he thought for an insane moment that she was the one who had started the fire—that Kathy had climbed out of the trunk and was burning the whole house to the ground. But Henry knew that she was dead—actually, irrevocably dead—and that not even her ghost would be coming back.

Downstairs Henry found his mom kneeling before the woodstove, tending to a small fire. She had probably forgotten to open the flue, and the smoke was curling back into the living room.

"Mom?" He rubbed his eyes. "What time is it?"

His mother didn't look up, "Go back to bed, Henry."

Henry walked slowly down the rest of the stairs. His head still felt groggy, like he saw everything a second after it happened.

His mom was wearing a threadbare robe with a long tear in the shoulder, right along the seam. She was holding a book in one hand, and was in the process of ripping out several pages, and feeding them to the fire.

"What are you doing?" Henry ran over to her and pulled her away from the fireplace. He pried the book out of her hand, flinching when she slapped his face. He clutched the book to his chest.

She didn't answer him, but hung her head and bent down to close the front of the stove. His mother stood up slowly and wiped her hands on her legs. When she drew her robe tighter around her waist, Henry noticed how thin his mother was—how sharp the bones of her face stood out in the firelight. He didn't know when she had gotten so skinny.

For one long, terrifying moment, Henry wondered if he was seeing his own mother's ghost. But then she went to him and put her arms around him.

"Mom?" Henry put his head on her shoulder. She smelled like smoke, but also like the perfume she always wore. Cloying and spicy—like flowers mixed with cinnamon. He pushed her away.

Henry flipped through the remaining pages of the partially-burned book, glancing at the familiar, handwritten words. It looked like only a few were missing. She must have just started to tear out pages when he came downstairs. He had come down in time—enough of it was left.

He realized in horror that he had left his book bag downstairs. His mother must have gone through it while he was sleeping.

"What were you doing?" he asked. Looking around the room, Henry saw the gun, and the box of bones on the coffee table.

Stupid bitch—Henry almost spat out those words, but managed to swallow them back.

"Mother, what did you do?" Henry's voice was thick, and he almost didn't recognize himself. He was so angry that he wanted to slam his hand down on the top of the stove so Sheila Grey could see the kind of damage she had just done. Make her see it on her own son's body. Henry brought his hand to his throbbing head and tried to shake those thoughts away. He felt dizzy.

When his mother finally answered him, she turned away—her bony shoulders stiff and awkward. She was crying, Henry realized. He couldn't remember the last time he had seen her cry.

"I was trying to protect you from him. From this world." She gestured to the books, and the gun on the table. Henry almost went over and picked up the gun, too, but fought the impulse. He couldn't threaten his own mother with a gun, and she would never use it against him. He was her son.

"You don't need to protect me from Richard. I can take care of myself."

His mother shook her head, but didn't speak for a long while. Long enough that Henry noticed the light starting to shine through the windows. It must be morning.

Finally, she spoke. "I know why your father killed himself. It wasn't depression. I wasn't having an affair with your uncle." That was one of the stories that went around—that Henry looked too much like Richard.

For a moment, Henry couldn't breathe. Which meant he almost couldn't ask the one question he had always wanted to know. Then he whispered, "Why?"

His mother looked at him with wide, sad eyes. "Because he thought there was a ghost inside him, and he was trying to save you."

Chapter Sixteen

"What do you mean Dad had a ghost inside him?" Henry's head started to ache as he spoke—a sharp throbbing in his temples. "Ghosts don't just climb inside people."

His mother scrunched up her forehead, like she was trying to figure something out. Then she reached out her hand. "Can I see the journal again?"

Henry took a step back, "Absolutely not."

"I won't hurt it. I just . . . I want to show you something. Something your father showed me before he died."

Henry didn't give the book to his mother, but he held it out.

"Open it to the first page," she said. "Look at the inside of the cover."

Henry did as she asked. The words, *Property of Eli Grey*, were written there. "Who is Eli?" he asked.

"Eli was your great uncle. He was insane."

Lies.

Henry shook his head. "I've never heard of him before."

"Eli died a long time ago. Do you remember the Accident? Eli was there. The reason no one talks about him is because your grandfather wouldn't let them. He didn't want anyone to mention Eli's name."

"Why?"

"Honey . . . your grandfather thought, for a long time, that Eli caused the explosion. That he was somehow responsible. And there were other rumors at the time. Missing women. Well, your grandfather just started to pretend that his brother had never existed."

Lies. More lies. A deep, seething blackness roiled up from Henry's stomach. He tried to focus on his mother's words, but his head hurt so much. "But what does Eli have to do with Dad?" Henry asked.

"Your father found this journal when he was a teenager. He became convinced that Eli's ghost was in his head. Alexander thought that Eli had somehow gone into his body after the Accident. And it just got worse. Your father said that Eli was telling him to do things. Bad things. Your father was afraid he was going to hurt you."

"Dad would never have hurt me."

"I know, honey. I know. But that's what your father thought. He would take out the journal and read it over and over again. The words made no sense. They were just crazy ramblings. Eli was a disturbed man. And your father, well, he was obsessed with him. In the end, well, I truly think he was trying to protect you."

"So it was my fault? I'm the reason he's dead?" Henry thought he would feel something when he said these words out loud—questions he had always wondered, but had never asked. But he just felt hollow.

His mom didn't answer at first. Her lower lip trembled when she said, "I didn't mean to blame you. That's why I didn't want you to know."

"But you do, don't you? You do blame me?"

"No," she said quickly, "I don't. I was just mad. Mad at your father. Mad at life. And I wondered . . . I couldn't help but wonder if there wasn't some truth to it. I looked for signs in you. Sometimes I thought . . ." she hung her head. "At times I was afraid. Afraid of my own son."

Henry stared at her.

"Can you forgive me?" she asked. Tears were running down her face. She looked so fragile. When Henry put his arms around her, he was uncomfortably aware of how breakable the bones that made up her ribcage were. How slight her neck.

Then Henry remembered Kathy's body in the trunk of his car.

"Mom," Henry whispered, not entirely sure what words were about to follow. "Something bad happened."

Henry's mother drove while he sat in the passenger seat, struggling to stay awake. It was probably five in the morning, and they needed to put Kathy's body somewhere that no one would find it.

"It was Richard," Henry had told her. "He killed Kathy. I think it was part of a ritual." Henry felt lightheaded, as though his words had been sky-written in his brain and were drifting apart like clouds. "I think . . . what if the ghost is inside Richard? What if Eli made him do it?"

His mother had just nodded like she had expected it—like it was just one more piece of their inevitable future falling into place. Then she said, "We have to hide her body. It will look like you did it."

It took them almost an hour to dig a hole big enough, back behind the overgrown shrubbery in Richard's front yard. No one would see them here. No one would ever look behind his uncle's big metal fence. They took turns shoveling. Even though they tried to be quiet, Henry kept expecting his uncle to come out of the house at any moment. Henry wanted him to come. He wanted Richard to see that they all knew what he had done.

It was his mother who wrapped Kathy in a blanket, and together they moved her body across the lawn to the newly dug grave. He could have summoned the ghost with the goggles (he still had the box of the ghost's bones in his book bag), but he didn't want to frighten his mother. At least, that is what the voice in his head told him.

As the dirt covered Kathy's body, Henry wondered why he didn't feel more—of anything. He just had an ache in his chest to do something. To go find Richard.

Finally, Henry couldn't wait any longer. He left

his mother to finish filling in Kathy's grave and let himself into his uncle's house. He pulled the box of the ghost's bones out of his book bag and held it up like a weapon.

He found Richard in his study. The room was dark, with just the soft, greenish light of the sun filtering through the leaves.

"I know your secret," Henry said, shaking the box of bones. "I know what you did."

Henry didn't really know what he expected. Perhaps that Richard would finally explain everything. Why he kept the bones of a dead man in his library. Why he killed Kathy.

Instead, Richard closed the distance between then and slapped Henry across the face.

He'd been hit by his uncle before, but never so hard. His head whipped backward and slammed against the wall behind him.

"Little shit," Richard growled. "You think you can just play at something you don't understand? You think you can just take my things."

Richard wrapped both hands around Henry's neck and lifted him into the air. Henry sometimes forgot how incredibly strong his uncle was. He gripped Richard's arms, as his uncle dragged him across the room. He tried to speak—to tell him to let go, but he couldn't breathe. His uncle lifted Henry up and pressed his back against a shelf of books.

Right next to the ghost with the goggles.

Henry could feel the ghost burning beside him. The edge of his vision lit up with the flames in the ghost's goggles. The bones rattled in their box—still clutched in Henry's hand, and the ghost flickered.

Richard relaxed his hold on his nephew's neck, but held him firmly to the wall. "Do you have any idea what you took from my house?"

Henry's head was pounding again—worse than it had ever been. He felt like his brain was splitting down the middle. He cried out, tears streaming down his face, but his uncle just shook him.

"Do you know what you almost did?" Richard said. He released Henry, snatching the box of bones out of his hand. Henry fell to the floor, his vision blurring. Next to him, he could sense the ghost turn its attention to his uncle. The air around them grew hotter—so hot that Henry swore the tears on his face would turn to steam.

There was a movement outside the window. "Henry?" a voice called out. His mother. She had probably heard the yelling and was coming to see what had happened. Richard turned toward the window, his back to Henry.

Henry saw an old paperweight that had been knocked from his uncle's desk in their struggle. It was shaped like a dog and was staring at him with its metallic, unblinking eyes. Henry reached out with a shaking hand and picked it up. As he gripped the small, metal dog, it began to glow just like the doorknob had earlier that night. Henry could hear something crackling in his ears.

He stood on unsteady legs and lifted the paperweight—ready to strike his uncle's head. Before he could bring it down, a scalding hand gripped Henry's wrist and twisted him around. The ghost with the goggles smiled at him. Henry screamed in pain. He could feel the fabric of his shirt burn against his skin, and the skin itself begin to blister.

Richard turned back to Henry, holding up the cigar box triumphantly. He opened the lid and scooped up the shards of bone. They filled the palm of his hand. Half of Henry wanted to pass out, and let the pain be absorbed by the darkness. The other half held Richard's gaze.

Henry didn't want to look at his arm, which had grown numb, like it wasn't even there.

"I won't let you do it," Henry said, though he didn't know what he meant by it, exactly. "I'll still stop you." He doubled over and threw up on his own shoes. He crouched there for what felt like a long time, shuddering and dry heaving.

He felt a hand on his back. "It's okay," Richard

was saying, "You're going to be just fine." Then Henry cried out in pain as his uncle pulled his arms sharply behind his back. The last thing he remembered before he passed out was the feeling of rope tightening around his wrists.

Chapter Seventeen

On Friday, Lorna woke in a terrible mood. She found herself frowning at her hands as she smoothed her stockings. She picked at an inflamed hangnail on her thumb, ripped it until a tiny bead of blood welled up.

Richard had come over the night before, but she hadn't enjoyed herself—not the way she had the first night they were together. This time, Richard had kissed her like he was trying to steal her breath, pressing her body to the mattress until she felt that the bones in her ribcage might snap. He seemed . . . untethered. It was like a part of his mind was somewhere very far away, and he had forgotten her small and very breakable body was even there.

Afterward, Lorna wanted to talk to Richard about her day—about the newspaper clippings she had found. She wanted to tell *someone* about the parts of her life that no one would think to ask about . . . the things that kept her from disappearing completely.

As he held her tight to his body and stroked the bare skin on her arm, Lorna found she didn't know what to say. His touch tickled, and she tried to shift ever so slightly until she could find a more comfortable position.

Richard whispered to her. He said that she was special. That she was going to help him make the world a better place. Then he gave her a bracelet and asked her to wear it the next day. It looked like it was made out of delicate pieces of white shell or ivory. He said he was going to need her help. It had sounded important—life and death. When had anything ever been that important in

Lorna's life? She was starting to wonder if Richard was quite sane.

He left late that night (or was it early the next morning?), and Lorna was left wondering what exactly had happened. She had thought it was going so well. That she might have met someone she could spend her life with. But now Lorna was left with the unsettling feeling that she had just slept with a stranger.

It started to pour down rain on the way to school. She had never seen clouds gather so quickly—the wind herding them across the sky like wayward sheep.

When Lorna arrived at school she found the students damp and bedraggled, and soon the room smelled like a combination of wet dog and soggy grass. Everyone was in a bad mood. By third period Lorna wanted to smother each and every one of her students. She was supposed to talk about the final days of World War II, but the children just kept talking over her.

"They're totally going to cancel the game," said one boy who was wearing a letterman's jacket. He didn't even bother to whisper. "This blows."

Lorna raised her voice. "Can someone tell me what date the war officially ended?"

Another guy spoke up, "I think I saw lightning. Ah man, they're never going to let us on the field in a lightning storm."

"September second," Lorna continued, talking over the top of her students. "The war ended on September second. Almost six years, exactly, from the beginning of the war."

When the lights went out, Lorna felt as though time had slowed down, turned back upon itself— like she already knew it was going to happen. There were a few shrieks, and then nervous laughter from the class.

"All right," Lorna said, standing up from where she had been leaning against her desk. "It is just a power outage from the storm. I want everyone to stay seated. Do *not* go near the windows." She imagined a tree branch shattering the glass and wondered if she should close the blinds. She gripped her hands together and turned the new bracelet over and over on her wrist.

"Miss Evans?" one of the girls said in a loud whisper.

"Yes?"

"I need to use the ladies room."

"Me too," piped up another girl.

"Just stay in your seats," Lorna commanded.

There was utter silence for a full minute as Lorna watched her class and the class watched her. Silence filled her ears until it became a hissing, rushing sound like pressing your ear to a seashell.

When Lorna was a senior in high school, they used to have duck-and-cover drills—as though their thin wooden desks could possibly protect them from a nuclear bomb. Still, as Lorna faced her students, panic began to grip the base of her throat.

Lorna began to wonder if she should tell them to get under their desks and cover their heads.

When the screaming began, Lorna flinched, but figured it was more nervous energy or some kids horsing around in the dark. But the screams didn't stop. They kept growing and spreading through the school, as fierce as the wind outside.

"Miss Evans?" It was the boy in the letterman's jacket. She could just see the outline of his head in the darkness.

"Yes?" She couldn't remember his name.

"I have to go." He pushed his chair back from the desk and was walking towards the door. "I just . . . I can't stay here."

"Stay in your seat!" Lorna snapped, hearing her voice grow shrill. The screaming kept getting louder, and she could hear running in the hallway. The boy opened the classroom door and was gone. And she still couldn't remember his fucking name.

Lorna hesitated for a moment. Should she stay with her class or go after the boy? Finally, she told the other students, "If you get out of your seats, I will wring all of your necks." Then she left.

The hallway was dark, and there were students running past, though she couldn't see their faces. Lorna wished she had thought to pick up a flashlight, but she wasn't even sure if there was one in her classroom. She jogged down the hall, trying to spot the boy's letterman's jacket among the students darting by. Someone slammed into her, and she was knocked off her feet, her head cracking against the floor. A foot stomped on her hand, and she cried out, scooting toward the wall.

She sat there—covering her head with her hands, listening to the pounding footsteps of terrified students. Then she smelled it. Smoke. It was faint at first—just a tinge of something acrid in the back of her nose and a faint stinging in her eyes.

Fire. The realization hit her like a slap in the face. She started to cough, and couldn't stop until her lungs felt bloody. Lorna's first thought was to run to the front door, then out to her car and drive home. Drive as far as she could from this school. This whole fucking town.

Then Lorna tried to remember the proper procedures. Surely there should be an alarm going off, and the students should evacuate the building. But the only sounds Lorna heard were the screams and the footfalls of children running every which way in the dark.

Lorna pushed herself up and pressed her back against the wall. The smoke was growing thicker, and she could feel heat on the left side of her face, toward the direction of her classroom. It was impossible to see in the dark and the smoke, but she could just make out an orange glow down the hall. When she heard the first real voice of the fire, the crackling and the whoosh of flame, Lorna ran.

She pushed her way through a mob of students who had gathered at the front door. Lorna elbowed and shouldered her way to the front, until her hand was on the handle. As the skin of her hand stuck to the white-hot metal, Lorna screamed.

Chapter Eighteen

When Henry woke up, he was at home in bed. His mother was sitting beside him.

"What—?" He tried to sit up, but his hands were tied to the bed. "What's happening?"

"Henry . . . " His mother began, placing a hand on his forehead. "It's to keep you safe. Richard explained it to me." Her eyes were rimmed with red. "Would you like a glass of water?"

Too late! Oh god, I'm too late! Henry didn't know why he was thinking those words, or why he was filled with bitter regret. It felt like someone had punctured a hole in his body, and he was draining out of himself. "What day is it? What time?"

"It's Friday. Almost noon. But sweetheart, like I said, Richard already explained everything. He's just trying to keep you alive."

"Let me go." *It wasn't too late after all. There was still time. Not much, but a few hours. Time enough to stop Richard.* These thoughts in his head cut through his skull like the blade of a pickaxe, and tears sprang to his eyes as his head throbbed and his vision blurred.

His mother shook her head. "I won't. I'm not letting you go." Her eyes filled with tears again, and Henry could see she was exhausted. "I'm not letting you die, too."

"Mother!" He struggled against the ropes. His shoulder still hurt, but was a little better. "Mother, this isn't your decision to make. You have to let me go. Now. Or more people are going to die."

She nodded. "I know, honey. But not you."

"You stupid bitch!" he shouted, pulling at his binds until his wrists started to bleed. "Stupid fucking bitch! I should have smothered you in your sleep. Let me go!"

His mother stood up and backed away from Henry's bed. There was a loud snap, and one of the wooden bars of Henry's bed broke away. As his mother stared down at him in horror, Henry untied his other wrist, and jumped out of bed, the rope still clutched tightly in his hand.

"Don't," she said, holding her hands out in front of her. "Don't do this."

"You made me do this," Henry heard himself say. "You should have let me go."

Quiet Henry—the Henry who usually waited in the back of his mind and watched—that Henry grabbed his mother by the arm and wrapped the rope around her neck.

Stop it. Henry thought to himself, feeling like he was in a terrible dream. *Stop it now.* But he couldn't stop it, even as his mother clawed at his arms. Even as her body went limp and collapsed to the floor. Even then he twisted the rope, until her lips turned blue.

Henry changed his clothes, putting on a clean pair of jeans and a new shirt. He watched himself get dressed, with his mother's body lying in a heap behind him.

Downstairs, Henry saw that the journal and the gun were still sitting on the coffee table, right where he had left them before they left to bury Kathy's body. He had to hide the journal. Someone might take it from him. Someone might try to hurt it again. His heart pounded at the memory of his mother burning the first few pages.

Hurry, said the voice while he frantically looked for a hiding place. *We have to hurry.*

When he was done, Henry took the gun and went outside. Not seeing his car in the driveway, he started to run through the pouring rain.

It would take him less than ten minutes to get to the school. He could still make it. He still had time. He glanced at his bare wrist as he ran.

Where is my watch? Henry thought, not sure why it was suddenly so important. *Where is my watch?*

Come on, come on, rang a louder voice in head, drowning out Henry's thoughts. *Hurry. We have to hurry.* As Henry ran, his mind went blessedly blank.

When he got to the school, he could tell the ritual had already started. He could see the flickering light of the fire in the windows. He needed to get inside. He needed to find Richard. Henry closed his eyes, and thought, *Where would he be?*

By the Door, the voice said—no longer a whisper, but as clear as if someone were standing beside him in the empty room. *He has to be by the Door.*

"Where?" Henry said aloud. "Where is the Door?"

Find him.

Henry ran, rain dripping into his eyes. He looked for an open window—somewhere he could get in. Finally, he found a broken window on the far side of the school, near the gym. He climbed in, almost slicing his leg on the glass. In the distance, he heard sirens.

He ran down the hallway squinting against the many fires that seemed to have sprung up independently in each room. It was the work of the ghost, he somehow knew. The ghost with the goggles. *William Evans,* the voice told him. *That fool.*

Henry had no idea how his uncle had created such a powerful Token, but it was doing more than just controlling the ghost. It was feeding him. Making him stronger.

"Where are you, Richard?" Henry yelled, but couldn't remember forming the words. "Where are you?" The smoke was so thick that Henry had to close his eyes. Somehow, he could still see—still make his way down the hall—now empty of students. They must all be hiding somewhere. Or burning. *He had to stop Richard. This was madness.*

As he ran, Henry kept seeing his mother's face, pleading with him. He kept seeing Kathy's body. Henry had a flash of a memory—he saw his watch shattering on smooth, round stones. He could feel nails clawing at his hands. Not just his mother's hands, but Kathy's as well.

Not now. Don't think of them now. Just run. Henry did what the voice told him. He ran. All around him, people were burning.

Not knowing what else to do, Lorna ran back toward her classroom. She glanced inside Mr. Bishop's room and saw what looked like a pillar of flame by the front desk. Her stomach turned, and she tasted bile. She kept running.

At first, Lorna thought that her room was empty, but then she saw the little forms huddled beneath their desks.

"There is a fire," she rasped, her voice shot from all the coughing and screaming. "You need to get up, now." Her hand was bleeding from when she ripped it off the handle, and it was curled in a sort of half-claw at her side. Useless. She didn't even really feel it anymore. "Get up," she repeated, and overturned one of the desks in the front row. A girl shrieked and scooted back into the arms of a girl behind her.

"We're going to burn to death!" Lorna shouted. At the back of the room, the wall was covered in flame. She got down low, trying to breathe beneath the smoke and made her way over to the window.

She tried to open the window but it wouldn't budge. "We have to break it," she wheezed, picking up a chair and throwing it against the glass. Lorna couldn't even hear the sound of the glass breaking over the roar of the fire. It was going to be too late, she realized, watching the fire multiply and consume the back half of the room.

"Come on!" Lorna shrieked, pulling one of the girls with her. "Get out!" She tried to lift the girl through the window, but she struggled against her and kicked her in the stomach. "Now!" Lorna shouted. "Get out now!" There was a loud whoosh, and the girl exploded in flame. Her brown hair fizzled into nothing, and Lorna could see her features cracking and blackening. Lorna could see her eyes burst.

The flame that consumed the girl whooshed up the side of Lorna's arm and neck. Lorna screamed, knowing that this was her last moment—the last sound that would come from her lips. She lifted her arm to her face and screamed, "No!"

And then it stopped. Lorna could still see the flames dance over her skin—licking over her strange bracelet and eating her clothes. But it wasn't burning her anymore. She stared at the bracelet in the flickering, wild light of the fire. It seemed to writhe and pulse on her wrist like a living thing, almost in time with the flames themselves.

There must be music, she thought suddenly—madly. *Music I can't hear.*

Lorna laughed—because what else was there to do—and then coughed and coughed as she breathed in the smoke. Was she dead? Was she a ghost? But she didn't feel dead. Her burns didn't even hurt anymore, but perhaps they were just too big a pain to feel.

She looked back at her students one more time, as they writhed and burned around her, and she ran out the door. Lorna felt light—her soul had burned to dust, but her body was still whole. She held her breath and ran down the burning hallway, looking in each room. Trying to find anyone else who was alive.

Henry found his uncle standing in the center of the gymnasium. He was holding his hands above his head, and his eyes were closed. The flames hadn't reached this part of the school yet, but it was just a matter of time.

"Stop it," he yelled to his uncle. "Stop the ritual."

Richard opened his eyes. In the dark of the gym, Richard was surrounded by an orange glow. "I can't. It's too late." Henry saw that Richard had his right hand clenched into a fist, and he realized that his uncle was holding the ghost's bones. He was making the ghost do this.

Henry raised the gun and pointed it at his uncle's chest. Even though he had never shot a gun, he had that feeling again that when he pulled the trigger, he wouldn't miss. "Tell the ghost to stop." Henry's voice echoed across the room.

"I wanted to save you from this, Henry. I had hoped it would be different for you than for your father. But Eli's too strong, isn't he? Even after everything I taught you. You'll never be free of him. I can see that now." Richard raised his hand and gestured toward the gun. In an instant, the gun was so hot that Henry dropped it. It spun away from him and toward the door.

"You can't stop me," Henry shouted. His head hurt worse than it ever had before. It felt as though a hand was reaching out through his skull. He doubled over in agony. "You haven't won yet." As he spoke the words that he realized, finally, did not belong to him, Henry saw a light out of the corner of his eye. A bright, thin line that flickered between him and his uncle.

Henry heard himself laugh. "See! It wasn't enough! The Door is opening!"

Richard shook his head, walking toward Henry. "You never did know what you were doing, Eli. That's why my father beat you. The Door isn't opening. It is accepting the sacrifice."

Henry screamed—Eli's voice ripping out of his throat. "Alexander killed himself because of you. Did you know that, Richard? Your own brother didn't think you could beat me."

"Henry," Richard shouted back, "if you can still hear me, you need to fight him. You need to run. Get out of here."

Henry's whole body was shaking as he tried to take control back from the quiet Henry. The angry Henry. The Henry that he now realized was never Henry at all, but was a ghost that lived in his head. Eli Grey.

He focused on his uncle's face. Henry trembled when he said, "I killed her. I killed my mother. I think I killed Kathy." He gasped a huge, racking sob and felt his body double over. When he stood back up, the ghost was back in control.

Richard's face was stricken. "You killed them? Sheila's dead?"

"Does it matter? You're killing hundreds of people. And for what? To put off the inevitable for another fifty years? I'll keep coming back. I will beat you, eventually."

"But not yet," Richard said, taking hold of Henry as he struggled to contain the ghost. Richard pulled out a knife and held it to Henry's throat. "I'm so sorry, Henry. I hope you can forgive me someday."

Another memory flashed through his mind's eye. Kathy's face beneath a veil of water. Kathy's eyes wide and frightened—staring up at him.

"Do it," Henry whispered, fighting to use his own tongue. "Cut him out of me."

Chapter Nineteen

Lorna saw two things when she reached the gym. First, she saw Richard holding a knife to his nephew's throat. Then she saw a gun at her feet. She picked it up and held it with her burned hand. Her father had taught her to use a gun when she was a teenager—one of the few useful things he had passed along to her.

"Let go of him," she called out to Richard. Lorna didn't understand what she was looking at— why would Richard try to kill Henry? His own nephew? But the world was burning around her, and nothing made sense.

"Lorna," Richard said, glancing from the gun to

her face. "Put it down. You have no idea what is happening right now."

Henry looked like he wanted to speak, but the knife was pressed so close to his Adam's apple that he might just slit his own throat if he tried.

"Drop him," she said again, bringing the gun level with Richard's eyes.

"You won't shoot me, Lorna dear. I know you won't. I have to do this." When Richard moved his hand, Lorna pulled the trigger. She screamed at the deafening gunshot, but her hands were steady.

Henry tried to scream, "No!" But it was too late. As his uncle died, his lifeless arms released him. As Henry watched his uncle drop to the floor of the gym, he felt the ghost take hold of his body again. He watched himself pick up the knife and approach the teacher.

"Are you okay?" Miss Evans asked him, lowering the gun. "Did he hurt you?"

When he sliced her arm, she dropped the gun. "What are you doing?" Her voice was a thin croak, and she started to cough. He wanted to stop—to let Miss Evans leave before the ghost killed her too.

Henry tried to pull his hand back, and was able to stop the knife, just for a moment. Just long enough, he hoped.

Lorna held her hands in front of her face, waiting for Henry's knife to strike her. When it didn't, she looked up and saw a figure standing behind Henry. It was Richard.

Richard's body was still lying right where it had fallen when she shot him between the eyes. But there he was also standing right behind his nephew. A bloody hole oozed darkly in the middle of his forehead. He reached out his hand, and took hers, just like he had that first day, after she fell asleep at school.

Time seemed to stop when he raised her hand to his lips. Then he vanished.

Henry growled and swung the knife toward her face. Lorna's instinct was to back up and cover her eyes, but she heard herself scream, "Grab his arm!"

Henry's arm stopped in mid-swing, and his face contorted into something ugly.

She took a step forward, and her head began to pound. "Take him to the Door," she yelled, pointing to the center of the gym. *Everything is going to be all right,* said a voice in her head. A voice that sounded exactly like Richard. *I'll take care of everything.*

Something Lorna couldn't see dragged Henry backwards, until he appeared to totter on the back of his heels.

"This won't stop me!" Henry shouted, struggling against his unseen captor. "You're still going to fail." Then Henry vanished. Lorna could just make out a thin, watery light where he had been standing. For a brief fraction of a second, Lorna saw another person standing in front of the light. Even though the man was wearing dark welder's goggles, Lorna knew he was looking right at her.

He smiled, and in that moment he looked almost exactly like her father. She stared at him, the tears she had refused to cry before coming unbidden to her eyes.

Then he was gone.

Lorna knew she needed to get out of there. She needed to run, and keep running. But instead, she stopped and, despite the tears running down her cheeks, smiled to herself.

She felt for the bracelet on her wrist and turned it around and around.

"I'm here, Lorna," she heard herself say. But it wasn't her voice. Deep in the back of her mind, she could hear Richard saying each word. "Everything is going to be okay. You'll never have to be alone again."